The Magic Pencil

The Magic Pencil

Karen E. Dabney

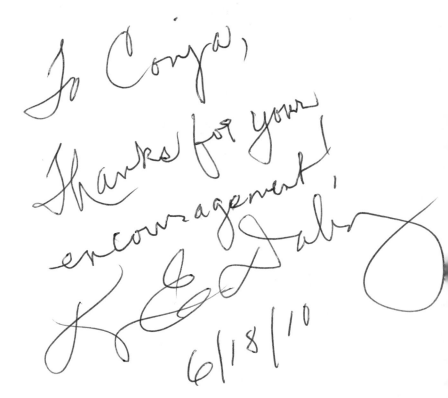

To Conya,
Thanks for your encouragement!
K. E. Dabney
6/18/10

THE MAGIC PENCIL

Dabs & Company, PO Box 47327, Oak Park, MI
48237-5027, USA
dabsandco@att.net
www.dabsandcompany.com

Cover design by Karl C Klein
karlklein@verizon.net

Book design and typesetting by Brenda Lewis
www.ubangi-graphics.com

This is a work of fiction.
Names, characters, places and incidents either are the product of the author's imagination or are used fictiously.

Manufactured in the United States of America

FOR OUR YOUNGSTARS

This story is about YoungStar Malcolm Bakersfield, his mysterious new classmate and a pencil that changes everything!

If you don't understand him at first,
Try reading aloud then you'll have a thirst.
'Malc' has something to say about everything,
Even if no one's really listening.
You might agree with him or have a different view,
It's OK wit him if it's OK witchu!
Now, read his story, then you'll see,
Malc's a lot like all, us, we.

Things are seldom what they seem —
once you see a pencil gleam!

Table of Contents

Prologue

Today is my brotha's birthday. I'm gettin ready to look for him when my mother calls my name. "Yeah, Mom?" "I want you to call Martin and tell him I made his favorite cake. Ask him what time he plans to be here so I'll know if he's coming for dinner."

"I'm just bout to go find him. He's probly up an out by now." It's one o'clock in the p.m. I figure he'll be at one hangout or another.

"Well, I guess you know better than I. If you can't find him at a halfway decent location — don't go looking for him anywhere else — *all right*?"

"OK. I'll be back after a while. Oh, yeah. Is Jam gonna be home in time?"

"He plans to be. He's rehearsing til about five. Depends on the time Martin wants to come."

"Ah'ight, Ma."

"Bye-bye brover. I lub you!"

I pick up my lil sista, kiss her an put her back down on the floor. She grabs at my keys cuz she wantstuh see my plastic *good luck star*. I let her jangle it against the keys an say: "Bye-bye to you too Jamilah Kibibi Hayes, and *I love you!*" Satisfied, she waddles back to our mother.

I get my bike from the basement an leave out on my way to Ole Jess Moon's house. That's usely the best place to find Martin. He's practicly livin there now. I ride for bout ten minutes an turn a corner. There he is — standin like a prizefighter — lettin the sun hit his face. "Hey," I say to him an Jess while bumpin fists together, "what up?"

"Hey, lil bro. Not too much. Jus chillin."

I see they been workin on a car in the garage.

"Malc, you ain tryin to grow now is you?" Ole Jess smiles.

I *am* gettin a lil taller. It feels good to hear it. "Tryin to do as much as I can, my man!"

"The way you growin you might git taller'n Martin!"

"Ah'ight now. Whatchu doin lookin for me?" Martin's dark eyes are tryin to pick my brain.

"Yeah, as if you *don't* know. Mom wanna know if you comin for dinner."

"She bake a cake?"

He's studyin me now like he's givin me a physical. "Ya *know* she did. Hey, you got a *real mustache* man!"

"Yeah. I'm growin too."

He scratches his head. I notice he's been to the barbershop.

"Tell Ma I'll come roun six. My man Jam gon be there?"

"Yeah, he's sposed to be. Aw, man, that reminds me! I had a dream that was off the chain last night! You know how I'm likely to fly an stuff in my dreams? Well, in this one I stay on the ground, an it happened round the time I started gettin straight *A's* at ole Gillespie Elementary. I hadtuh grab a notebook an write the main parts a it down while it was still fresh. Everybody was in it! It seemed so real — but magical too! Martin, I was wantin you to stay in school an stuff, man!"

"You *must've* been dreamin! But I have thought bout takin up computer design or somethin. Jus thinkin now cuz you know I always an — *all ways* — got some bidness goin on! Why you laughin Ole Jess? Everybody ain gon work out they garage forever for a penny an a pint!"

"Man — I was laughin witchu — not atchu. Nothin but the best for you, Martin. You too Malcolm!"

"Well," Martin chuckles, "c'mon Malc, out wit it. Tell us all bout this dream a yours. Seems it must be kinda special."

I'm glad my brotha always takes time to listen to me.

"Whatchu say bout it, Jess?"

"I'm *all* ears." Ole Jess grins.

"That's cuz you a ole elephant!" Martin snorts.

"An I gon member you said that too!" Ole Jess laughs an winks at me.

"OK, OK!" I break in, "I'm ready to tell y'all my dream! Like I said, most a it took place at Gillespie. I remember how crazy we was over pencils.

Maaaaan …

Chapter 1

Pencilology

Everybody likes the look, the feel an the size of a brand new, never been used pencil. An that pencil's even better when it's sharpened to a *serious* needlepoint. The teachers always be sayin: "*Don't run with a pencil! You could injure someone!*" So we run anyway cuz danger's just a game to us. But back to the point — ha, ha. It's best if you got a pencil that comes from someplace other than school. You can feel cooler than the kids usin them ole, free, yellow jobs. But if it is yellow — you still cool long as it don't have the writin on it that the school pencils got. An it should be a *number two*. Everything I ever heard bout pencils asks for a number two.

Now I know most kids don't be thinkin deep bout diffrent stuff as much as me.

See, I like to study things. Not just reglar things — like in school. I mean I like to watch people, animals an machines. Some a the kids I run wit call me *The Watcher* after the dude in that ole movie, *The Brother from Another Planet*. All he seemed to do was check everything out like a witness or somethin.

Yeah, I get into pencils just like most a my homies — but deeper — cuz I *watch*. The reason I do is cuz some kids be actin like a new pencil is gold! Even the ones who got they own! When the teacher busts out a new box — you'd think it's everybody's birthday! Which is weird cuz it's the *same ole* school pencils — only *new*. Kids be tryin to act all cool an unimpressed but they watchin every move of the lucky one who gets to sharpen them pencils. Sharpenin is a whole nother story cuz some teachers got *electric* sharpeners!

I know I talk a lotta junk cuz I hang round older kids an even some adults. I manage to pick up a whole lotta ways to talk. Ole school an new school — it's all the same to me. Conversatin an communicatin's what it's all bout.

We had a substitute teacher — Ms. Kady — for a week that tried to teach us how to *properly use pencils*. It tripped me out at first but she was OK so I listened. She said when she was in school the teachers showed the kids where an how to hold a pencil! She used a fat piece a chalk to demonstrate:

"My teachers would explain we were to lean the pencil back into the space between our thumbs an pointer fingers, in a *slant*. When the pencil lead became flat on one side, we'd turn it to the side that wasn't. There was less waste, less sharpening, and less reason to get up."

Boy, I knew wasn't *nobody* goin for that! Ev-ery-body wanna sharpen they pencil at lease once a hour! Who even want they pencil to last longer than the eraser? The pencil be all stubbly an stuff. An those add-on erasers look wack. I ain never had a teacher — before that one — talk bout the right way to write — ha, ha. She said she hadtuh *graduate* to usin special ink pens in fourth grade! We can't even use ink pens at my school! Too many kids be needin correction fluid all the time.

Since I been watchin, I've seen some things bout pencils that probly never will make no sense. Like playin *leads* or *breaks*. That's when you an your partners try to see who can break whose pencil lead — or even the whole pencil — first by thumpin each other's. I don't even know why we do it!

Maybe cuz we bored, wanna show off or cuz it drives the teachers nuts. It's sorta the same way wit erasers. The teacher gives us nice new pink erasers. Sooner or later those erasers become *history*. It starts wit us puttin our names on them. Then some kids draw on them, stick they pencils into them, break or cut them in half, so now you got the crumbs developin. Course small pieces a rubber make good *projectiles* as Mr. Burns — the math teacher — calls them. So we end up throwin them at each other! After a while, hardly nobody got a eraser an those that do *might* share — or most likely won't — cuz now the erasers is *real* valuable! Then we get reminded by the teachers bout how we *abused* the erasers when we had our own.

Speakin a ownin — it always be the kid who do the lease work wit the most pencils! This kid's usely a boy. How he collects all them pencils is a bit of a mystery. He may've brought a few wit him, stole a few — he feels anything that hits the floor is fair game — might've got one from the speech teacher or lied an tol another teacher he needed one. Somehow he ends up wit bout fourteen in diffrent sizes, lengths an colors. He usely keeps a fat rubber band round them an displays his catch all day. You got a better chance a growin wings than gettin him to loan you one. An he hardly ever do any work or even draw! The one we got now don't talk in class or do nothin. We call him *The Collector*.

Now, at most kids' homes pencils an erasers be hard to come by. An — even if you got pencils — you usely ain got no real sharpener. This explains another kinda behavior: kids tryin to use the class sharpener — if it works — before they go home. Course some kids have they own hand sharpeners to bring back an forth — as long as they don't get lost, stolen or taken by the teachers for various reasons.

At my house we always got pencils an a real sharpener

too. Part a why is cuz my mom likes to write poetry an stuff. She wrote a poem bout me. It goes:

"My Child

My child is my hope.
I keep him safe from dope.
I hug him everyday,
An bless him when I pray.
He's growing very strong,
And he knows right from wrong.
He is great company.
I raise him to be free."

I memorized it cuz it makes me feel good an I can say it to myself when I want to. I ain never tol it to nobody — cept my granma — til now. I guess my mom is why I like to watch an learn new words.

An write.

Chapter 2

Responsibilty an Cousins

I wake up earlier than usual an feelin great! I got a hunch that somethin real special is gonna happen. An it's gonna happen to *me*! My mother knocks on my bedroom door. I open it: "*Yes, ma'am,* what can I do for you this fine Saturday morning?"

"Good morning, *sir*! I'm on my way to the grocery store and should return within an hour or so."

That's 'Mom Code' for: *Get up and do your chores and finish your homework if you want to go with your father to visit your cousins.*

I bow to my mother. "Yes, my *liege*." She chuckles on her way out.

I do my chores an am just finishin up my homework when she gets back home. "Hey Mom. Is it anything else to bring in?"

"No, sweetheart. Thanks. Help me put these things away."

"*All right*! You got one a them pizzas! Can I have some for lunch?"

"OK, mister. Set the oven for 375 degrees and put the pizza in this pan. It should be ready in about twenty minutes."

"OK." I grin an bow out a the kitchen backwards.

"Malcolm, did you take out the garbage?"

"Oops! *Madam*, do you realize how *difficult* it is for *Responsibility Man* to admit to making an error? I will correctify the oversight immediately and it shall *never* happen again!"

"Right. You don't want to be put back in the dungeon. And it's *rectify*."

"Rrrrrright Momma!" I pick up the garbage bag, bow again an exit through the side door.

While the pizza's cookin I get on my brotha's computer — lef here by my him from some program he was in at school — an ride the Internet. I put in a search for black race car drivers. There's a lot more a them than I thought! I know some bout Willy T. Ribbs from my father. I decide to read bout Mr. Ribbs so I can showboat later.

There's a whole bunch a stuff bout Ribbs an other racers! I write down some a the site names so I can print out the info later. Like my mom says, I might be able to use my interests for schoolwork. I eat some pizza — just enough to get stuffed — then continue wit my readin.

When I hear three familiar car honks I jump up — hug my mom — an run out to join my dad.

At my cousins' there's always a lot to get into. There's three a them — all boys — an they close to the same age. Robert, Jr., Napoleon an Kevin is always ready to entertain each other but when I come over, they all try to entertain me at once! It's usely fun but I have to speak *standard English* cuz my Aunt Linda insists on it. She's my dad's younger sista an a teacher. Even though she has a Jamaican accent, she's always correct grammar-wise. She explained all this to me when I was bout six. She made real sure I knew where she stood.

When we reach the McIntosh home everybody greets us at the door. Then all us boys pile into the basement. 'Bobby' is the oldest at twelve. 'Leon' is nex at ten an 'Kev' is almost eight but he looks more like he's nine-an-a-half!

First, we get on the X-Box an play games wit it for over an hour. Then we start wrestlin. It's OK cuz we in the play area a the basement. As long as nobody mess up they clothes or break anything, we cool.

I'm on the team wit Leon an we called the Eradicators. Don't ask me what it means cuz I forgot. I just know it says we *tough!* Bobby an Kev are the Destroyers. We all got the runnin commentary goin: "In this corner is that amazing team, The *Eradicators!*" I holler.

"And in this corner is the favorite, The *Destroyers!*" roars Bobby.

All four of us tussle an break apart when our imaginary official gives a warning.

I have to keep tellin Kev to stop usin his fists. "No, Kevin, we're wrestlin, not boxin! Ow!" We all keep wrestlin til we out a breath.

Tired a that, we play a game I learned a long time ago called Monster in the Haystack. I'm usely the first monster. I stand funny an make ugly faces an growl: "Monster in the haystack, bing-bang-boo! Don'tchu laugh, don'tchu smile, don'tchu show your dirty, greasy, yellow teeth!" That's the spell. I pick a victim an the chosen one has to keep a straight face. He's got to have his mouth closed an uncovered, eyes on mine an make no sound while I'm doin my best to get him to laugh or — at lease — smile.

Accordin to the rules the monster can't touch the victims at all, an the ones left can laugh at the monster an the chosen one. I decide to start wit the easiest one first. I flap my arms an get up real close to Kev an say *bluh, bluh* over an over as if I'm Dracula bout to take a drink from his neck. Course, he can't handle it an falls out laughin. I nex go to Leon, do a silly dance an pretend to eat somethin from inside my nose.

I get right up in his face — he's ready to laugh any second now — an offer him some a what I pretended to find. He covers his mouth an is out. I save Bobby for last cuz he — bein older an all — is usely harder to break up. But I got a secret weapon. I wobble over as if I'm gonna fall on top a him! He don't even move while he watches me. Then I act like I'm gonna kiss him! He jumps up an shouts:

"*Is you crazy!*"

I laugh an laugh wit the others until Bobby's laughin too. "Good thing your mother didn't hear your language, cuz!"

"*Shut up*, Malc."

So now it's Bobby's turn to be the monster. In his version we can't show our "*decayed, crooked an dilapidated teeth.*" He makes quick work a his brothas just by dancin around an tellin stupid jokes. When it's my turn I try to be stone-faced. Bobby gets me back real good. He gets up in my grille an acts like a mad dog that's gonna bite my nose off. It's more annoyin than funny — but it works. We let the younger ones have a turn an really frustrate them cuz we don't break. When they quit we crack up from all the stuff they did. Then they feel better.

Uncle Robert calls us to come eat. We run up the steps an slow down at the doorway. Then we eatin some homemade beef patties, a salad wit all kinds a vegetables in it, an some spicy cabbage. We hungry after all our playin an my aunt can really cook! She introduced me to curry goat wit rice an peas. I'll never forget how good that first taste was!

When it's time to go, one thing that's hard for me was bout to happen. Aunt Linda hands me a big bag. It's full a Bobby's clothes that's too small for him an too big for Leon. Bobby an I avoid each other's eyes an I thank my aunt politely for the gifts. I can sure use the clothes — an they usely fit — but it makes it plain they famly's doin *waaaay* better than mine. Bobby's ole clothes always look almost new, not your usual hand-me-downs. I'm glad they don't give me the ones wit fancy labels on them no more. I don't wanna have to fight over some ole designer's name again. I shake Uncle Robert's hand an kiss my aunt's cheek, then me an Dad hit the road. I tell him more a what I learned bout motor sports, then an now.

Neither of us mentions the bag a clothes.

Chapter 3

The New Girl

It's a new week an there's a new girl in my class. I don't pay too much attention to girls cuz they pay too much attention to me. But the strange thing bout the girls is most a them like me even more for ignorin them! I do talk an play wit them some at lunch time, though. I guess they like me cuz they think I look good. I think I look OK. My mom's friends always say how handsome I am. They specialy like my eyes an my "*looong* lashes." I feel kinda shy bout it cuz they grown folks an talkin to me like that.

Yeah, I get good grades an usely stay out a trouble but I ain that well behaved neither. I just know education is important even if some a the stuff we sposed to be learnin don't seem so.

Anyway, this new girl acts diffrent. She's friendly but not like she wants you to think she's so fine an all that. The first day I asked her if her name meant somethin special. Her name's Nia. It's African for "*purpose.*" She's chocolate bar brown, got big hazel brown eyes an *dreadlocked* hair down her back. She's a lil on the chubby side. On her first few days in class some a the kids laughed at her but Nia looked right through them. Days later she got girls playin wit her hair an askin questions bout it. Just from the way I feel when I'm watchin her, I guess I havtuh say I really like her.

Nia's real talented. She writes too an can sing pretty good. She read me a poem she wrote:

"Happy to be Nappy

Like me hair the way God made it,
Don't even have to comb or braid it.
Nature does my hair for me.
Locking is my way to be.
You may not think it good for you,
Expressing yourself is your right too."

Nia speaks *"proper"* English bout ninety percent a the time. We tease her for it cuz where we live you only do that if you can or havtuh! Some a my friends couldn't do it if they tried! Well, maybe when they readin out loud — ha, ha.

I call myself speakin two languages: standard English an what some people call *Ebonics.* I don't like that name cuz it sounds like a *joke.* My mother says *"Black Relaxed Language"*— cuz every culture has its own style. (Sometimes I tease her and call it *"slanguage!"*) For us it's the way most African Americans can speak or usely understand when they hear it. My mother an my Auntie Evelyn taught me the diffrence tween the two. When I use standard English, I hardly ever slip up. An my schoolwork shows it. (Wonder why it ain called *American.* When I watch anything wit folks from England talkin, I can hardly understand them — specialy they slang!). Well, I just like to speak the way most everybody in my hood do. Mom says it's OK as long as I know when to switch up.

She tells me stuff like when she has a customer at work — no matter what color they are — she waits until she gets a cue from them on which *code* to use. When she gets a white customer, she usually speaks standard E then. She also explained to me how white people — just like every-body else — got they own different way of talkin. We hear it so much on TV that we might think any way whites talk is right. One example is *you guys* is like sayin *man* or *y'all*. We usely say *man* an *y'all* to girls an boys, men an women. Whites seem to say *guys* to everybody. A lotta blacks say *guys* too. Another example: blacks might say *don'tchu* an whites might say *don'tcha*. But the flip side a that is when white people try to speak cool *our* way. As soon as they take some talk a ours an make it they own, we usely start sayin somethin entirely diffrent. Rap music, hip hop, TV, an movies seem to be chan-gin that though. I guess it's a good thing.

Well, Nia never slips up when she speaks out in class but she sounds sorta like everybody else when we outside playin. I watch her an know she should be called *The Thinker* cuz she is a deep one. She don't seem to notice me watchin cuz she usely be thinkin hard.

I notice she's diffrent in other ways. For one, she don't care what her pencils look like! They got bite marks an they stumpy wit paint chipped off an no eraser to speak of! But no matter how messed up her pencils be, Nia always do *excel-lent* work in school. Teachers who notice how bad her pencils look give her new ones. Wittin a day or two, those pencils be dogged! I'm guessin it's cuz she's such a serious student, writer an artist.

Now, I don't really compete wit Nia but I start workin harder in school to get more *A's*. An I show out some to get her attention. My mama notices my graded schoolwork is up an she's real happy bout it! She asks me who am I tryin to impress. I just smile.

Nia's freehanded too. She shares books, ideas, candy or whatever. Needless to say, nobody wanna borrow any a them raggedy pencils! She got a notebook that she scribbles in — yes, scribbles, her handwritin ain too good — an draws in every free minute. She made a *slammin* picture for me a four boys playin soccer cuz I tol her I play it sometime. Too bad we ain gotta art teacher no more.

All the teachers allow Nia to do as she please in her notebooks an go to the library or computer room whenever she wants cuz she's considered *gifted*. She even skipped a grade at her ole school! Sometimes I think that'll happen to me. My mom says she don't know if I'd be ready for that *responsibility*-wise. She also thinks I'd be too busy gettin into the other kids' bizness. No hurry, I guess. But Nia — she fits right in wit us! Nobody even knew she was younger til she accidently tol somebody. She said she didn't want us to be upset. By the time we found out — nobody seemed to care.

I see some a the books Nia be readin from the public library an I think she could probly hang in eighth or ninth grade. At lease for readin. Gillespie's the only elementry schools that still goes up to sixth grade in the city. I bet Nia'd be real bored if she didn't get to leave class when her work is done. Sometimes she goes to help Mr. Shine in the kindergarden class where she's a Future Teacher.

Well, I knew there's a lot more to find out bout Nia but I had no idea how much there wastuh know.

Chapter 4

A Discovery?

A week later, I find myself desperate for a pencil! I know where I lef my new ones — right on the kitchen table. Ms. Winston — the homeroom teacher — is givin us a English test first thing! An she *never* gives out pencils, cept on Wednesdays when we trade our ole ones for new ones. She says that would teach us to be more *responsible*. Yeah, *that word*, again.

Nia's already tossed her raggediest pencils in the trash. She's got two lef an they ain much better than the ones she tossed. I don't think any a her ole pencils is good enough for tradin. Anyway, nobody else got a spare — cept The Collector — an I don't wanna give him the satisfaction a shakin his head *no* to me. So, I choose one a Nia's pencils. Course she allows me to take the lease raggedy one — which ain sayin much. I smile an thank her. She smiles back at me an I swear it's the most *beautiful thing*! I feel all stupid goin back to my seat, like I'm in one a those sappy movies or somethin! I guess I like her more than I thought cuz I feel like I'm blushin. Good thing it don't show. Maybe she's the special thing that sposed to be happenin to me!

I feel even more strange while takin my test. I pick up that ole pencil — touch it to my paper — an *it starts to glow*! I look it over. Just your average, raggedy, pencil. I take a quick look around to see if anybody else saw what I think I saw. Nobody seems to have an the pencil ain glowin no more. But when I begin to write, my thoughts come easy an the pencil moves as if it's readin my mind! I don't even need the eraser! It's actualy a lil scary! *A magic pencil*? I stay quiet but I wanna tell *everybody*! What if I had just imagined it, though? Yeah, maybe that's it. I finish my test.

Just before it's time to go, I ask Nia if I can keep the pencil. Course she says OK.

But I forget to take it home.

Today I find out I aced that English test. I got the second highest score in the whole class! You already know who got the first. Actualy, I don't feel too happy bout it cuz I didn't really study that much for it. I figured I'd get at lease a *B*, tops. Maybe the pencil *is* magic cuz how I ended up wit a 99 percent is a mystery to me! English ain my best subject. I like to write but I hate followin all those rules! My mom tol me not all great writers follow them but they're good to know — just in case.

Mom's had some a her poems an stories published in a few magazines. Sometimes she even gets paid for them! She keeps copies a her stuff in a special notebook. She tol me that if the time came when she could make a livin as a writer, it'd defnitly be a dream come true.

I really admire my mom an watch how she tries to write everyday, even when she's tired from workin. When I go to bed, sometimes the last thing I see is her hunched over writin at the dinner table or usin the computer. Mom's always been writin an had even planned to go to college years ago but all that changed after my brotha Martin was born. I wonder what would happen if she had a magic pencil? I decide not to tell her anything about my experience because she wouldn't believe it anyway. I'd havtuh have proof first.

Well, all this mornin, the pencil makes everything I write *golden!* We even get to have free drawin time right before lunch. I draw the best picture I ever have of a super sonic jet plane! Two a my boys almost get into a fight over it. I give it to Nia.

Now the pencil is bout half the size it was when I got it — due to my goin to the sharpener too much. I couldn't help it — the teacher got a electric one!

When I use the pencil after lunch the same thing happens witout the glow. *The pencil is bringin out the best in me!.* I sneak looks at Nia to see if she knows her pencil is transformin a good student into a great one! Bout the tenth time I look up, I see her lookin into my face wit that same beautiful smile. I get the movie feelin again but this time the whole room freezes! There ain nobody movin or talkin but me an Nia!

She's still smiling an says:

"I really appreciate what a good friend you are to me, Malcolm. I usually have a hard time making one so soon."

"You made it easy to do, Nia. And it's nice to have such a smart person as you in the class. You're someone I can use my twenty dollar words with and you understand everything I'm saying. Even when I'm talking '*slanglish*, — ha, ha! An me an you both know it don't mean you stupid if you be talkin that way!"

"I know xactly whatchu mean, Macom!"

"Just being able to be all of yourself and say how you feel about things that most folk in your crowd wouldn't appreciate — is cool. And not havin them look at you as if you're crazy for even thinking about certain things."

Nia is noddin her head an smilin at everything I'm sayin.

"I'm so glad we had this chance to talk about being friends.

I can be really hard to get to know. Thanks Malcolm."

When she turns around in her seat, everything starts back up an the class is actin as if we hadn't spoke at all! The only way I can explain what happened is what my mother calls my *extreme imagination*. But I have a real hard time convincin me that I was daydreamin or somethin this time. I'ma try usin the pencil at home tonight.

Up til now, girls was never that important to me. An Nia is becomin *real* important. *An she is defnitly not your average girl!*

I try to write a poem about her:

> *Nia's pretty cool.*
> *She's a new girl at my school.*
> *She's got dreadlocks on her head.*
> *Yeah, that's what I said!*
> *She's good looking too,*
> *And probably smarter than you.*

Nah! I tear it up an throw it away.

When I get home, I take out the pencil an get ready to start on my homework includin the two extra sheets Ms. Winston always gives me. Everything comes easy until I get to a story problem in math. I even need my calculator to figure out the answer! I pick up a homework sheet for English that's bout the proper way to use commas. But I havtuh keep lookin in my English book to do it too! Now I'm thinkin the pencil only works in the classroom. Well, I gotta do my homework anyway. At lease it's a challenge.

I'd be bored stiff if is wasn't.

Chapter 5

Humor

I'm just kickin back when the phone rings. It's one a my best friends from school, Kenyon 'Kenyo' Frazier. "Yo, Mr. Frazier, what's the haps, man?"

"Not much Mr. Watcher. Whatchu doin?"

"Nothin man. Just did my homework an was thinkin bout what to get into."

"Well — since you ain doin nothin — come over an stay for dinner — my treat!"

"What's on the menu, Mr. Frazier?"

"Man, just come, ah'ight? Ain nothin special. Moms asked if I wanted to have you over since she ain seen you for a while. Course I tol her *'no'* but she insisted."

"Okeydokey, Mr. Frazier. I will inform my business manager of our intentions and will see you in thirty." I call my mother at work.

"Munger's Pharmacy, may I — "

"Hey Mom, it's your wonderful, youngest son calling to get permission to go to Kenyon's house for dinner. His mom requested that I come."

"Who is this, now?"

"Your outstanding, youngest son!"

"Oh — of course — my *modest* son. Yes, you may go to

Kenyon's but I expect you to be home by seven-thirty."

"*Roger that!* Thanks."

"You're welcome and *thank you* for calling."

Mom has a good sense a humor an I'm *always* tryin to make her laugh. Sometimes she pretends not to be amused but I can usely tell when I get to her. I think I was successful this time.

I arrive to Kenyon's an lock my bike to a pole in his backyard. We play wit his big, black dog, Taboo til it's time for dinner. I'm bein treated to fried chicken, coleslaw, cornbread, an greens. Ms. Frazier asks me an Kenyon how'd the greens taste. Course she waits til we'd ate what was on our plates. She's busy wipin food off the toddler twins — Nelly an Arthur — when me an Kenyon give our *seals of approval.* She tells us the greens was made wit smoked turkey by Mr. Frazier before he left for work. I knew Mr. Frazier made some *mean* barbeque but I didn't know he actualy *cooked!*

For dessert, we have cookies an chocolate marshmallow ice cream (my favorite)! Ms. Frazier even gives me a plate a food for Mom. I thank her an ride home balancin the plastic covered plate wit one hand.

When my mother gets in she is most pleased to find a fresh home-cooked meal waitin for her. She heats it up an enjoys every bit.

"How'd you like the greens, Ma?"

"They were delicious — just like everything else. Why?"

"Mr. Frazier cooked them with smoked turkey. I thought you'd like to know."

"Malcolm, I hate to burst your bubble but I've been giving you smoked turkey greens and such since you were a baby!"

"I knew bout the spaghetti. What bout Granma Sil? She's been usin turkey too?"

"Yep, she sure has. That's how I learned to do it. Smoked turkey for *sauerkraut*, ground turkey for *tacos* — matter of fact — I hardly ever give you pork, period."

"What bout when we have pizza an barbeque?"

"OK, you got me there. It's really hard to resist then."

"*Yeaaaaaah, Mamaaaaaaa!*"

"OK, Mr. Silly, that's enough."

One a these days I'm gonna surprise Mom wit a meal. Only thing stoppin me is I don't know how to cook!

The nex day I make sure I bring the pencil back to school. Uh huh! It makes the day's work an stuff easier to do again. Now I'm thinkin it only works its magic in school. I still don't tell nobody bout it. It's hard not to, though. I get through the a.m. tryin to catch Nia's eye. Other than the smile I got when I first came to class — nothin.

Out on the playground we talk a bit til Nia gets up to hang out wit some a the girls. Shoot! I was just bout to ask her if the pencil *is* special. I decide to wait an see if she brings it up. By dismissal, I still don't know. But I do remember to leave it at school.

My mother's home when I get there. She didn't havtuh go to work all day. Soon as I walk in she tells me to wash my hands an come into the kitchen. I guess she wants to teach me some bout cookin. She's been readin my mind again! I come into the kitchen an look at the stuff spread out on the counter. "Aha! This looks like the makins for spaghetti!"

"You are correct, my son. And since I've decided it's time for you to learn how to cook some basic things, you and I are going to work together. Now, we're going to cheat and make this dish in the simplest way because the real way takes a lot of time and patience. OK, we have two unfrozen tubes of ground turkey. Notice that one says *sausage.*"

"Check."

"We also have water almost boiling in a big pot, a box of spaghetti noodles, a white onion, three cloves of garlic, seasoning, and a jar of spaghetti sauce.

I've already filled the large pot with water — about two inches below the top — and let it sit on high. We let it keep heating until it boils. In the meantime, we wash off the turkey tubes, cut one tip off the ends of the packages and *squeeeeze* the turkey onto this big plate.

We mix the meat together, season it and turn it into flat ovals about this size. After that, we peel the onion, keeping our mouths closed — so the onion doesn't make us cry too much — then cut it up into small pieces."

I havtuh blink a few times cuzza that onion. Mom continues:

"We peel the garlic cloves by removing their outer shells. Then we chop each of them up into about seven or so pieces.

We now put a small amount of oil into the frying pan — just enough to coat the bottom of it — and place the onions and garlic in first and let them *sauté.* Wash your hands again so the garlic and onion smell won't be so strong on them.

Now we put the meat —"

"*Meatbovals!*" I name them.

Mom smiles an plays along.

"— meat-*bovals* into the pan with the eye on medium. In about three minutes, the meat-*bovals* will need to be gently turned so they'll get brown all over. Is the water boiling?"

"Yep."

"OK, keep watching the turkey. Now, gently flip the meat-bovals over. You can use a fork along with the spatula to do it. Don't worry — it's OK if they don't stay exactly in shape. So now, we wash and rinse the sink and put the colander in it."

"Check."

"We put about half the box of spaghetti into the boiling water but first, we carefully break the noodles in half so they won't need to be twirled a lot when we eat. You may skip this part because it's a bit hard to do it right. So, we put the spaghetti into the pot and allow it to boil for ten minutes. I'll set the timer."

"OK."

"How's the turkey doing?"

"Brown all over."

"Turn the eye for the turkey off and sprinkle a little more seasoning on it."

I do. The timer *dings* an Mom taste tests a noodle.

"They're done. Now, we put on the oven mitts and slowly pour the spaghetti into the colander to drain off the water. This particular brand doesn't have to be rinsed off. Now, you put the meatballs — I mean meatbovals — garlic and onions into the pot the spaghetti was in and add the sauce. Careful, don't let it splash. Put the eye on medium and *gently* stir the sauce around a bit."

Bout five minutes later she says:

"OK, now we slowly pour the spaghetti into the pot — again stirring gently — then put on the lid and turn the eye down to low so it will simmer. Oops! I forgot to add a bay leaf. There! It should be ready in about fifteen minutes! Make sure you stir it gently a few times, then turn the eye off and let it sit."

"Should I set the timer?"

"Sure."

"Mom?"

"Yes?"

"Do you expect me to remember all this?"

"Not this first time but you'll remember some of it and when we do it again, you'll remember more. And the third time you should be able to solo with me watching! I'll be back before it's time to eat. I've got to get Ole Dusty an oil change."

"OK, *Ms. Mom*." After I stir the ingredients a few times, I hear the ding. Then I turn the eye off. Don't want the *turkghetti* to burn. I start on my homework so I can watch TV later. A program's comin on in a hour that's bout animals.

Huh. My mom got me cookin. Reminds me a doin a science experiment.

Chapter 6

Better Days

OK, so now I'm gettin the attention a all my teachers cuz I'm *"consistently doing A work"* as I heard Ms. Winston tell Mr. Thayer, the assistant principal. I'd finaly mastered the slant an roll technique wit my pencils so they last longer. I use the one Nia gave me for tests an quizzes only. I ain sure if I wanna ask her for another one yet — but I get her to touch my three new ones just for luck.

I'm even doin better in gym. The coaches be slappin me on the back for my performance an sayin, *"You got it, Malc!"* That's what most people call me. Nia's the only kid who always calls me Malcolm.

Me an Nia talk bout all kinds a stuff. She's the first girl I ever talked bout sports wit. I tell her I'm thinkin bout joinin the after school basketball program an that maybe I can get some a my friends to join. Kenyo is always thinkin bout it. Our school don't have *no* teams for *no* kinda sports. That's why this program is right on time! I don't think none a us is that hyped to stay at school a extra hour but it'd be a cool way to get better at the game an hang out.

Nia an me also talk bout our names havin meanins. All I know is that I'm named after one a my heroes, Malcolm X. "I can look in my auntie's book on baby names so I can find out what my name means."

Nia says:

"I'll look for an African name for you in book I got from the public library.

Did you know there are so many languages and *dialects* in Africa — because it has fifty-three countries — that no one can actually tell you the number? America can fit into the continent of Africa *three times!*"

Nia's name comes from the *Swahili* language. She thinks it's the most well known one here. I tell her I want a Swahili name too.

"OK but meanwhile, you'll have to find out Malcolm X's other names at different stages of his life an beliefs".

"How many did the brotha have?"

"At least four that I know of."

My mother's got the movie about him. It's real long. I've seen it twice but I can't remember any a the other three names for my man. Lessee, I can get a book — probly got the info in one a my mom's books — or try the Internet. I'll find out an surprise Nia when she asks me.

I'm always up for a challenge.

Today, I use one a my *good luck pencils*. Partly cuz the one I got from Nia is almost a nub an cuz I need to be sure the others work. We got a spellin test to take an I feel no fear cuz I can spell an never miss more'n one word — if that. I ain too suprised when the pencil seems to flow along like the one I got from Nia. It don't glow though.

Course, I get 100 percent on the test. I'm glad I can stop usin the almost nub — but I'm gonna save it in my utility box anyway. I begin to feel sorta guilty an wonder if I should try again to ask Nia bout the phenomenon or tell anybody else.

I decide to try somethin at the end a class.

My bud Juan Lee — we always call him by his first an last name cuz he looks Chinese — is down in the dumps cuz his stepdad didn't take him to the movies over the weekend. His real father got shot when he walked into a store while it was bein robbed. He was killed *instantly,* an Juan Lee was *only five* when it happened! Anyway, his stepdad's always disappointin him over somethin. He makes Juan Lee feel he's actin like a baby if he complains. Juan Lee's grades be shaky sometimes — but it ain cuz he don't care. It's cuz his parents party too much an he can't study or sleep good when they do. He had tol me:

"I actualy like it when they leave me alone all night."

We used to have a after school tutorin program that Juan Lee could've kept goin to but the money for it was cut so it ended after three months. I decide to give him a pencil to cheer him up an as an experiment. I give it to him an say: "Forget bout your famly situation. You can come study wit me if you want. I can ask my mom if you can spend the night at our place when things is really out a hand."

He grins an we bump fists. I wanna tell him I know it's hard for him haventuh to raise hisself — but that would be gettin too deep in his bizness. Far as I'm concerned, Juan Lee's the *only* grown-up in his famly.

I return to my seat an I notice he's sittin up taller. I'ma ask my dad to give me some a those ear plugs he uses at his job for Juan Lee.

I feel good.

Chapter 7

Protection

I'm wonderin how Juan Lee did on his homework. He had said there wasn't nobody to help him if he got stuck. Both his mom an stepdad — Mr. an Ms. Taylor — is the type that just got by in school, so even if they wasn't drunk an available, they wasn't gonna be much help. My momma tol me they both had a hard life growin up — an even harder luck. She remembers them before they gave up strugglin an it was downhill after that. Things hadn't been much better for Juan Lee's real father, either.

I tol Juan Lee to think a somebody he could call for help wit his homework. I knew this was part a what he'd havtuh do in order to really learn the assignments. Me just givin him clues wasn't gonna help him learn. I want him to do better by findin ways to help hisself. Sides, I don't have the patience it takes to teach.

When we see each other in the hallway, Juan Lee is excited! I didn't walk to school wit him today cuz he was late — which hardly *ever* happens. He shows me his work an it looks good! Ms. Winston decides to let us check each others' papers. I make sure I get Juan Lee's. When the checkin is over, I have my proof. Juan Lee almost always mess up his homework an usely the best he'd get wuz a C. This time he got a *B!*

When I first saw his homework I asked, "Juan Lee, did you have help?" He squinched his eyes an said:

"Sorta. I tried real hard by myself, first. Then I called my Uncle Mark when I had a question. He helped but teased me bout askin: '*Since when you start carin bout your grades?*'"

I know it's real hard for Juan Lee to ask for help. Maybe the pencil made him feel it was OK. Maybe it works on how you feel too? After we pass the papers back to the owners I look back an see my boy smile.

At lunchtime, Nia asks me how Juan Lee did on his assignment. I look at her funny an ask why.

"I know you tried to help him, Malcolm."

"He got a *B*."

"Cool!"

I watch Juan Lee shootin hoops an he seems to have more confidence. On the way back to class, I tell him; "Hold onto that pencil cuz you don't wanna jinx your good luck."

He nods his head seriously.

At home I think bout how there's a down side to gettin older — an good grades — in school. It's harder to walk cool then — specialy if you a male. Cuzza my achievement — I get teased, mean looks, an havtuh go through stuff like my cap bein took an tossed around like a baseball. This treatment's nothin compared to what happens to other students. Kenyo an me talk bout one a the latest victims on the phone:

"Yeah, Malc, I know they got fourth grader Pauline Clifford yesterday. I saw her on the way home. She showed me her broke glasses. She was pushed around in the bathroom by some older girls til they fell off her face. She said she didn't cry, though."

I feel myself gettin real angry: "See, man. That kinda stuff goes on all the time! Did they hurt her or take anything?"

"Naw, she's ah'ight."

"Good. I know she's pretty tough for her age."

"Stupid bullies ain got nothin better else to do. Most a them be the kids who don't wanna learn nothin. I'm sick a them tellin me I'm a sell-out an *actin white* cuz I do my schoolwork."

"They need to focus on they own biz. Quit tryin to get us to join the club. But I think most be scared to try to do better."

"Yeah, like if they don't try, they don't fail."

"Some do got serious problems, though. A free lunch's probly all they get out a school. My father tol me sellin out really is: *don't try* to learn nothin, *halfway go* to school, an *drop out* mentaly — then physicly."

"*You know.* Sometimes I wish my parents would cut me some slack bout school."

"Mine be on me bout it too. But it's all good, homeboy, cuz we can actualy *plan* our future! Ain too many kids round here talkin bout goin to college."

"I know, man. I can just picture it. New girls to meet — "

"Ma says everybody don't gotta go to college. Some kids do good gettin a job after high school an work up to bein a manager or more. Some go to a trainin program an make it that way. But she feels if you got a chance to go to college, try it, cuz it might be your thing after all. An — if you can't go — you can learn a lot jus by readin."

"My parents say '*There's dignity in all positive work.*'"

"That's like my man, Mr. Skye. To be the school janitor, cool wit us, an do his job right too! He's married, got three kids an *my* respect. He holds a smile for everybody an calls us kids his '*young stars*' even though most treat him like he's the school slave. Lease he got a *real* job."

"Yeah, Mr. Skye *is* cool. Lease he ain out there sellin drugs like Sherona Wicks' famly do."

"Yup." I try not to think bout Martin.

"Shooooot, man. I'ma get me some scholarships so I can go *away* to college!"

"Me too man! Play sports for a Big Ten school. Livin on campus would be real cool!"

"Dang, man! Do you gotstuh make everything rhyme?"

"Just can't help it most a the time."

Remember when I said I usely stay out a trouble? I forgot to mention I got some help in that area. I don't havtuh worry too much bout bein a target at school cuz I'm cool wit a lotta the olduh kids in the hood. I also got protection in the form a my brotha, Martin. He's named after *Reverend Doctor Martin Luther King, Jr.* It's funny, cuz the only time Martin looks for peace is when he's worn out from runnin the streets all week!

Last year, Mom had enough a his rowdy behavior an sent him to live wit his father. Martin's dad hardly ever be home so Martin can do whatever he wants — like only makin guest appearances at school. Anyway, he's got my back cuz I'm his brotha an he always says: *"Stepbrotha don't mind steppin up for his brotha."* He's only fifteen an got some a the olduh boys at his school terrorized!

He tol me a while back: *"If it makes you happy to get good grades, Malc, I'ma see that you do. Jus cuz I don't care bout school don't mean you ain got to. Some a us jus can't deal wit all the rules an regs, know what Ah'm sayin?"*

I wish he'd give school more of a chance or at lease get a G.E.D. He ought a go to college but I know better than to even bring that up — just like my suspicions regardin his *activities*. I figure they might be somethin I'm better off not knowin bout. But Martin always drops by the house every so often just to make his presence known an to give Momma a hug.

Somethin else bout when you got protection, it kinda covers your boys too so me, Juan Lee and Kenyo havtuh act a lil tougher round school an the neighborhood.

Me an Juan Lee reach his house first. Mine is one block away on the same street. Today I'm gonna ask his mom if he can study wit me at my house. When we get to his door he tells me to wait an goes inside. He comes back an lets me in, holdin his finger in front a his mouth. The whole house is dark but I can hear somebody snorin. Juan Lee turns on a small lamp an I see his mother layin on the couch. There's a bottle that looks like some wine or somethin an a lotta cigarette butts in a ash tray on the coffee table. Juan Lee pulls out a piece a paper an writes a note. I guess he's lettin his mom know he'd be at my house for a while. He puts the note on the table wit a corner under the bottle. Then he motions for me to go to the door. We go out quietly. Juan Lee locks the door — it wasn't locked when we got there. He looks at me cuz he's feelin shamed. I touch him on the shoulder an say nothin.

We walk on to my house.

Chapter 8

Famly

I t's a perfect fall day, like the Indian summers my granma talks bout from when she was a kid. She remembers trick-or-treatin wit only a sweater over her costume. An the *worse* thing that could happen was your bag a candy gettin snatched!

Now kids havtuh have they candy inspected by the police an stuff. An you best be careful who you open your door to if you passin out treats.

My mother don't even *like* Halloween no more. She only lets me go to the rec center or to private parties to celebrate it. One time I asked could I go wit Kenyon to t-or-t in the suburbs. From what I'd heard, that was the best way to get good loot! My mother said *"no"* an she was a lil angry bout me even askin.

Later she argued:

"What, you think candy from the suburbs can't be poisoned?"

I tol her I guessed so but I knew it was botherin her for other reasons cuz she had a lil frown on her face for a while. I think it's cuz she wishes we lived in a better, safer neighbor-hood. I think it's cuzza her pride an all.

My dad's comin to get me soon. He an my mother still get along, they just couldn't live peacefully together so they got divorced. I usetuh let that really upset me but then I think bout Martin an Juan Lee. They dads just don't seem to care at all.

Today my father is takin me to the movies. Sometimes his new wife goes wit us. She always waits in the car at my house. She ain wit him this time so Dad comes in an has a lil convo wit Mom.

"How are things with you, Carolyn? Our boy still doing well in school?"

"Everything's good, Richard."

I'm sittin there all up in they bizness cuz I still wish they'd get back together. But then, I remember the yellin an cryin an door slammin an think it's best they don't. Sides, Mom's boyfriend, Jam, is pretty cool an I get to go places wit him too. When he had a motorcycle he let me ride on it twice. That's how he met my mother cuz my Uncle Walter worked on his bike.

Later, Jam sold it cuz he was worried bout his legs gettin hurt. He tol me: *"I need my feet to keep the beat!"* He's a drummer in a jazz band. I been to see him play a few times. He an Mom been together for almost a year. I think they might get married; then *I'll* be a stepson. I wonder how many steps I'll havtuh climb before I feel *really* close to *Mr. Jamal Musa Hayes.*

Dad stands up, kisses Mom on the cheek, an asks me:

"Ready to ride, boy?"

"Yep." I kiss my mom on the other cheek.

She smiles an says:

"See you tomorrow, son."

Bittersweet is how I feel when I'm wit both a them together.

My dad's name is Richard Bakersfield, Jr. but everybody calls him

Rich. Makes me wonder if he got a stash a cash somewhere — ha, ha. He's tall — six-two — an we share the same deep brown color. He was born in Jamaica an came to the U.S. when he was 21. He's got large hands an is usely doin somethin wit them.

Dad's almost always smilin an in a good mood unless you press him, then you get to see a whole nother side. His car is kept good but it's bout two years ole. He an *new wife* live in a *noice*, big apartment in a tall buildin. I figure he's doin ah'ight. He works for a construction company. New wife works too at some office somewhere. They don't have any kids yet. I wonder how I'll feel if that happens. I'm already a lil jealous cuz I'd get to see my dad more often if it wasn't for her — I mean Aurora. I'm glad he an I alone this time.

The movie, *Kung Fu Hustle,* was *cool!* It had lotsa martial arts action! Becuz it was in Chinese we hadtuh read subtitles. I did pretty good at keepin up. But you don't havtuh read everything to understand the story. It had a lotta funny parts too. Dad wasn't too happy bout it bein so violent and all. But I've seen a lot worse on video games!

My dad likes watchin foreign — an ole — movies. He says you learn somethin bout other cultures an times that way. I do the same thing by readin mythology an folktales.

We had passed up gettin refreshments cuz we gonna eat some fast food *"garbage"* — as Dad calls it — later. Fine wit me. Mom don't like me to eat much junk food.

After eatin, we go to the park an toss a football for a while, then Dad shows me some more moves wit a soccer ball.

"You're getting better, son."

I feel good an play harder, pretendin to be Freddy Adu. "Dad, where's Freddy Adu from again?"

"West Africa. Ghana, I believe"

"He's still just a teenager, right?"

"Yah, *mon*. Before him was Pele, ya know."

"Yeah? Where's he from?"

"Brazil, South America."

"Is Pele his real name?"

"No, and I can't remember what it is."

"Accordin to the Internet, there's another soccer man from Africa that's really popular. Do you know his name?"

"You might mean George Weah. He's from Liberia, West Africa. And there's also Steven Appiah and Michael Essien who are up and coming. They're both from Ghana too. They all may get to play professionally in Europe."

"Is Liberia a African word? Sounds like library."

"No. It comes from the ancient Roman language called Latin. The country was named Liberia because freed black people were sent there from here while most blacks in America were still enslaved. The word is also where the English words book and library come from. Liber means free."

"Do you think Barack Obama has a chance to become president?"

"Yes, son. He has a very good chance," Dad smiled.

"I'ma get Juan Lee an Kenyon to come play soccer wit us one day. OK?"

"*Irie*. The more the merrier!"

I don't know any other kids who play soccer. I'll bet my dad would teach it at the school if he had more time. He enjoys sharin his knowledge. I like the way he just knows things. He's always joggin my brain an introducin me to one thing or another. I don't even mind him playin his *reggae* music on the way to his home. I'm kinda likin it too now.

I wonder how two men my mother was wit could be so

diffrent. Course, I mean my father an Martin's father. My mother says she was very immature when she was goin wit Martin's dad, Eddie Davis.

I feel a lil sorry for Martin. He hangs out mostly wit men an they treat him like he's already grown. Dad gave him a standin invitation to hang wit us if he wants. Martin smiled like he was cool wit the idea but he tol me later he had other things to take care a. He'd thanked my dad an loped off down the street. His lope is one a the things that *really* gets on our mother's nerves.

Mom worries bout Martin a lot. I heard her an Auntie Evelyn talk bout how he's almost sixteen an will surely drop out a school when he is. Sometimes Mom hastuh go to his school cuzza him bein truant. The only thing that stops her from givin Martin's father any trouble, is that he at lease got a home to go to. But I think it's also cuz my mother still got legal custody a Martin. He can't live wit my Granma Silver cuz she says he ain the boy she knew growin up. An Martin's Granma Elease moved back to South Carolina after his Granpa Ed died. I think if Uncle Walter was home, Martin could live wit him an Auntie Evelyn.

Sometimes I hang wit Martin at his house an his dad'll come through. "Mistuh Eddie" looks like he some sorta *playa* an real busy. It seems like his cell phone rings every five minutes! He an Martin favor cept Martin's a bit shorter an not mean lookin. Mistuh Eddie pays the bills an gives Martin money for food. I can tell they don't like each other much. Eddie keeps a lock on his bedroom an always seems on the edge, like he might pop any second.

Martin says his *pop* — ha, ha — brings a lot a diffrent women over an they all act like they seriously in love wit him. But Eddie just uses them until they become '*a problem*'.

Me an Martin still keep respect for females cuz Mom

brought us up that way. My dad never seems to disrespect women. Jam don't either — far as I can tell. Anyway, I know my mother wouldn't be wit him if he did.

Martin tol me he hastuh leave the house when his father's doin bizness wit somebody — whatever *that* is.

I suspect they don't see each other too often. I believe Martin's dad only lets him stay there cuz he an my mom got some kinda money agreement over child support.

By the time me an Dad finish our hangin an reach his home, Ms. Aurora has been there for a while. She's tall an deep brown too an she kinda looks like my mother somehow when she smiles but she seems shy an quiet. She reminds me a the beautiful sculpture of a African woman Nia showed me in a book.

"How are you Malcolm?"

"I'm good, especially since I'm with Dad. How are you doing Ms. Aurora?"

"I'm well, thank you."

I always remind her in lil ways how important my father is to me. It's still takin me a while to warm up to callin her 'Mom Aurora' cuz I feel weird callin her that. Mom, Mother, Mama, Ma, Moms, only means one person to me for now.

The nex day, Dad an me go to the barbershop. I like it there. The diffrent smells, the usely all men party an the special attention I get just for bein *"Rich's boy."* The men always be talkin an jokin bout everything under the sun. A lotta the jokes go over my head an I always wanna ask what they mean but my dad don't appreciate me buttin into adult conversations. I do get to play checkers wit him or one a the other customers most times though.

Today I notice a man wit locks an ask my dad did he ever think bout doin that to his hair.

"Nope. You think just because I'm from Jamaica, I should have dreads?"

I say *no* an then I tell him bout Nia.

"She sounds like a special, special young lady. You like her a lot, eh?"

"Yeah," I mumble. Then I say, "Maybe I'll try lockin my hair. I think it looks cool."

"Well, son, I'm not saying you should or shouldn't but it's more than a notion, *seen?* You have to be all spikey-haired for a long time and I don't think your mom would like it."

"Maybe when I'm older."

"Yep, maybe then."

When we reach my home I hug my dad hard.

"What's this, now? *Yah tink yah nah go see yah faadah again?*"

"I'm just glad to have a real one."

I get out a the car an run up the steps.

Chapter 9

Chuch, More Famly an Brain

Dang, I was sleepin good! Havin one a my superhero dreams where I could do anything! My mother hastuh shake me several times to wake me up. Why did Dad havtuh bring me home last night? Now I *gotta* get up an go to church! When I'm wit my dad, he leaves it up to me whether or not I go wit him an Ms. Aurora. An usely, I *do* choose to go. I just hate gettin up early on my days off from school. "Ow, my eyes!" I grumble when Mom raises the shade an the sun comes floodin in.

"Get up, son. You want to have breakfast first, right?"

I clean up an get dressed an wish it was one a those days when my mom didn't go. Then it'd be easier to get her to let me sleep in. We have a quiet breakfast an go to *chuch*.

The church my mom an me usely go to is kinda big. If she sends me by myself, I go to the smaller one that I can walk to. We like attendin either one. Today we go to the closer one cuz Mom is low on gas. We arrive while the choir is singin an others is just sittin down so we aren't actualy late. The pastor had chose for his sermon the meanin a *responsibility*. I can almost hear my mother willin me to pay close attention to the man. Pastor Freddie DuBois explains that he ain just referrin to responsibility to God, he's includin to ourselves an each other.

"The Good Samaritan was someone who knew that, indeed, we are our brothers' keepers. But the way things are today, one might — and understandably so — fear to do as much. However, there are many ways to be responsible to others and not just our kinfolk. Some ways are doing charity work, mentoring youth, being a friend to the elderly, and so forth. Do you encourage young people when you see them doing right? Do you thank others for every kindness? Do you try to brighten the day of someone who works in the service industry or do you just walk away without a thank you because they get paid to do whatever they did for you?

Our responsibility could be looked upon as trying to make the world a bit better for everyone. Small acts such as those I just mentioned go a long way. However, if any of you need a little help in this direction, I can *specifically* use some assistance in the soup kitchen. Please see me after the service.

You see, even I am performing a *service* right now. Do I expect to hear a thank you from each of you as you leave? No. *Your presence is my present!* But I certainly wouldn't mind a thank you. Lets me know you like what I do on a personal level. We can *all* use encouragement and appreciation. They help keep us walking in the right direction.

We are responsible for each other in many ways *simply because we are human*. We all need each other. And always remember: a little goes a long way! Take care of yourselves — and yours — and do what you can for others. A candle loses nothing by lighting another candle. Let the *chuch* say *amen*."

The service continues an when it's over folks seem to really be takin what Pastor said to heart. It looks like everyone is thankin him today as we go out. *Past the pastor as he's countin the sheep* I find myself thinkin.

In the afternoon, we meet up wit Auntie Evelyn (I keep forgettin to ask her to look up my name in her baby name book!) an baby Charlotte at Granma Sil's house. It's a two famly flat an Auntie Ev an Charlotte moved upstairs from Granma right before my Uncle Walter hadtuh leave cuzza the war.

There's a lot to eat an I do more'n my share. I also speak my best standard E cuz *Grandma Geraldine Silver don't play.*

"So Malcolm," Granma begins, "your grades have gone up, I hear."

"Yes, Grandma, I'm really working hard. I'm learning a lot every day. And I'm trying to become more *responsible* and — yes — I still enjoy school."

"*Hmmmph*, I should hope so! Education is the key, young man, and don't you forget it! Keep your eyes on the prize!"

"Yes, Grandma."

"How's that brother of yours doing?"

"He's OK. I see him every now and then. He looks good."

My mother smiles at me. Her skin is a deep, warm brown just like her eyes. Granma is almost tan wit dark brown eyes that seem to see into your brain — just like Martin's. Auntie Evelyn is almost as dark as me wit hazel brown eyes like Nia's. Baby Charlotte is what some people call "yellow," very light-skinned. It's too soon to tell what color her skin an eyes'll stay. I am the darkest person in the room. My mother calls me her "brown bear" an Martin is her "chocolate child." Uncle Walter is Granma's "caramel candy" and my mom is her "coffee with a drop of cream." So many colors in one famly. I tug at Charlotte's lil hand an say the poem my mother wrote bout her when she was born:

"Just know she's pretty,
Certain she's sweet.
Congratulations for giving
The world such a treat!"

Auntie Evelyn smiles and Charlotte squirms in her mother's arms as if she knows what I said.

After our early dinner, I go to the special cabinet where Granma keeps things for me to amuse myself wit. It was already made plain long back that these things would stay when it was time for me to go. Some a them had been used by *her children;* Mom an Uncle Walter.

I'm always grateful that as I get olduh there's more challengin toys an puzzles. But most a my favorites are the oldest ones. There's ole books an almost mint condition comic books on *Spiderman* — the first teen-aged superhero — *The Silver Surfer* an *The Black Panther.*

I still pull out those green army men from way back. But I don't play wit them for now. They make me think bout *Walter Silver the Third* haventuh go overseas cuz he's in the Air Force Reserves. I think I miss him as much as Mom, Granma an Auntie Evelyn do. But they eyes usely water whenever his name is mentioned. Sometimes I can't look at the pictures a him in the house, specialy the one where he's got his uniform on.

I mean to write to him but I don't know what to say.

When we get back to our house, me an Mom change our clothes an go for one a our two weekly walks. We walk fast cuz we walkin for exercise. Mom brings her five pound weights an I get the long stick for stray dogs. Mom holds her forearms up, hardly movin them wit the weights in her hands. Sometimes we trade. We usely walk to the library an back. That makes our walks bout two miles each.

My mom is five feet, seven inches tall. I'm almost to her chin now. I wonder if I'll end up as tall as my dad. Mom thinks I will cuz I'm kinda on the large side when it comes to my hands an feet. An Uncle Walter is bout six-one. Mom and me don't talk for a while until I say: "How tall is Jam?"

"Oh, I think he's five-eleven."

"Almost six feet. I wonder if I'll be taller."

"You will be at *least* six feet, Mr. Bigfoot."

We get to the library an turn back toward home.

"Mom, do you think you an Jam'll get married?"

"Yes, I think so. He's very sweet to me and I like the way he takes an interest in you boys."

"Will you have another baby?"

"That I'm not so sure about. It depends on if — and when — we get married. Are you looking forward to a younger brother or sister?"

"I guess it'd be OK. I'm old enough now where I might be some help."

"'*Might be*?' What's that supposed to mean?"

"Aw, Ma, I'm just teasin you."

"So are you still keeping up all those *A's* I've been getting used to?"

"Yeah."

"Cause you know, *A's* are pretty easy for a mom to get used to."

"I know! Such *responsibility*!" We reach our porch an both a us take a seat. Mom removes the scarf from her head an pulls her fingers through her short, curly hair.

"Hey girl, how you doin?"

It's one a Mom's friends walkin up toward the house.

"Hey yourself, Lucille!"

"Hey to you too *Mr.* Malcolm!"

"Hi Ms. Jones." *Here we go.*

"Carolyn, look at your son gettin handsomer an hand-somer every time I see him!"

"Yes, he does tend to do that, doesn't he? Gets it from my side a the family. I usely don't let him come out too much cuz I'm scared one a these overgrown lil girls gon swoop down an carry him off!"

"OK, ladies. I'm going into the house now, so you may continue your visit. All I ask is that you change the subject, *please.*"

"Why *certainly*, Mr. Malcolm. Nice to have seen you."

Ms. Jones an my mother been good friends since I can remember. When they get together, it reminds me a the girls at school. I like the way my mom slips in an out a her languages wit friends when I'm around. Pretty soon she an Ms. Jones is gigglin bout another subject an I'm free to listen to some a my CD's before I get tol to rake the leaves.

At school — durin lunch — I start tellin Nia bout my famly an ask bout hers. She answers:

"I live with my mom and dad. Mom's a massage therapist and Dad's a college professor. There's not much else to tell except there's a lot of family."

"How many?"

"Too many to count. We don't all live together but some-one is always visiting.'

"Any brothas or sistas?"

"Nope, just other relatives. Most are children."

"Don't, uh, doesn't that make it hard for you to do your homework?"

"Not really, because I have my own room — of course —and

can close the door. Or, I can use the study upstairs and close that door too. I'm pretty good at tuning things out; kind of like meditating. Now that's enough questions, Master Bakersfield!" She laughs.

Nia's laugh is one a the things I truly like bout her. I kinda wonder why she ain closer to any a the other kids like she is wit me. They all seem to like her — specialy my buds who think she's real cool for bein a girl an all. I still haven't asked her bout the pencil an she still behaves as if nothin's happenin.

Back in class, I get out one a my new special pencils an start to answer the questions to a story we read last week. I softly hum a lil song I made up while writin: *Comprehension and retention, tested almost everyday. I can do it, nothing to it. Everything will go my way.*

Our class is real quiet cuz Ms. Winston is angry bout how we lef out the room on Friday when the bell rang. The kids in the Safety Patrol an Future Teachers is allowed to leave ten minutes before the bell. So, after they lef, the kids who havtuh meet lil bros an sistas got up an got they coats. Soon as the bell rang we all lef— not waitin for permission. *"Weekend on the brain syndrome"* is what Ms. Winston called it. My guess is it bein so close to Halloween too.

Outside, after school, I see Nia an smile. "Which way do you go home?"

"A different way than you. Sometimes I take the bus and sometimes I'm picked up by a family member. I live too far away to walk."

There goes that plan. Nia suddenly reaches into her pocket, pulls out a cell phone an says:

"It's my mother."

She's the only kid wit a celly that I didn't know bout cuz she don't flash it around like the others who got one. We say *bye* an I catch up to Juan Lee.

Later, I finaly remember to ask Auntie Evelyn to look in her baby book for my name. She says Malcolm means *royal* or *prince*.

Well, all right!

Chapter 10

Letters

The nex day, I drop Nia a note askin if she would help me write a letter to my Uncle Walter. I just can't get myself to do it. I can't seem to find the right words to say. I don't wanna mess up an ask him things that might make him or me sad. Bein in a war ain like it looks in comic books or movies. It's *real* life wit *real* people dyin! I know Uncle Walter's ain gonna tell me all bout what he actualy sees or does. I wanna write him anyway just to let him know I miss him an care bout him. Nia had said she'd love to help me. She's sure anything I write would help make him feel good wherever he is an whatever he's doin. All my homeroom work was done an Nia was finished wit hers too. I ask Ms. Winston if I could go wit Nia to the computer classroom. She gives me a written pass an off we go.

There was already a class in the room but two computers wasn't bein used. We sit at the one farthest away from the class. Nia pulls a chair nex to me an I begin to type:

Dear Uncle Walter,

I look at Nia.

"I suggest you write it like a normal letter; pretend you're writing to me."

"OK."

> How are you doing? I'm sorry it has taken me so long to write but I have been thinking about you. Everyone here is doing well. We all miss you very much.
>
> I'm doing excellent in school! I'll send you a copy of my latest report card so you can see all the A's. I'm thinking of joining the after school basketball program and I'm still in the Checkers to Chess and Science Clubs. Halloween should be fun. I'll be at the recreation center again this year, I guess.
>
> I have a very good, new friend. Her name is Nia. She's cool and we have a lot in common. I can talk about anything with her, which is great!

Nia giggles into her hand.

> So, what is your job in the Air Force? Is it mechanical maintenance like you were doing in the reserves? Do you miss your real job at Motorcycle Mania?
>
> Anyway, I just wanted to say hello and that I hope you are doing well. I'll be looking forward to hearing from you.

Do you think I should say love?"

"Sure. He probably needs to hear that now as much as possible."

"Yeah." I finish the letter.

Love, your nephew,

Malcolm

I leave enough line space between 'nephew' an my name so I can sign in between them like a real bizness letter.

"See, it wasn't that hard." Nia whispers. "I think you did a wonderful job! Let me know when he writes you back."

"Thanks buddy. You know, this will be the first time I wrote a letter to go overseas."

After the letter prints out, we return to class.

When my mom gets home I ask her for Uncle Walter's address. She smiles an says:

"Oh, you wrote to him! That's thoughtful of you."

"Yeah! Nia was there to help me figure out what to say but I used my own words."

"*All right!* Here's the address, a stamp and an envelope. Mmmmmmah!"

I look in the mirror so I can wipe the lipstick off my forehead. Huh. I made my mom happy by writin her brotha a letter. Til now, I never thought bout how wonderful a good letter can make you feel. I'll write Uncle Walter again in a coupla weeks. Maybe he can get E-mail?

But I think letters are more special cuz you actualy touch them.

Chapter 11

More Proof

In math class I see Juan Lee workin away, his straight-haired head bobbin to his own beat. He don't seem to worry as much as he used to before I gave him that pencil. He's usin another one but I know Nia picked it up an gave it back to him when it rolled off his desk.

I smile to myself an get down to bizness. I notice Nia gatherin up some a her pencils an papers to throw away. One pencil is kinda long an still has a eraser. She tosses them in the trash can; all possibly magic. I'll ask her later why she got rid a the longest one.

Soon after, The Collector gets up from his throne, goes to the trash can an retrieves that very pencil. He returns to his seat, squeezes his hulky body back into his desk an continues doin nothin. I look back every now an then to see what he does wit the pencil. Sometimes he breaks one in two just to show off. *Uh oh,* he's movin. He touches the pencil an starts to add it to his collection. But he stops an pulls out a sheet a paper instead. *And he uses the pencil to write somethin on it!* I wonder if anybody else is seein this. I wanna *shout* but I settle down.

The excitement rises up again an I can't help myself cuz I'm so curious. I havtuh fake throwin away some trash so I can pass by an see what The Collector is doin. I take a peek an see his name on the paper along wit some math problems! It's a miracle! I mean, The Collector had become one a those kids destined for a special school. Every teacher who has — an had — him try they best to motivate him this school year, an nothin works. Psychologists, psychiatrists — you name them — Terry Evans sees them. His parents won't agree to havin him put in a LD class. I think they tryin to get him in another school.

Students — an some a the teachers — is a lil scared a him cuz he's so big. Durin the end a fifth grade, he just stopped talkin an workin in class. I know a lot bout his bizness cuz I was in the same class wit him last year. This year I overheard Mr. Norman — the social worker — on the phone while I was waitin to deliver a note from Ms. Winston. He was talkin to somebody about Terry's behavior. But Terry sho is doin somethin now! *Man*, I wish I could watch him longer!

At lunchtime I tell Nia what happened.

She smirks:

"Maybe he was inspired."

"He was using *your* pencil," I say seriously while looking to see where The Collecter was standing. He didn't do much during lunch time either.

"What pencil?"

"The one you threw out that was still kinda new. Why'd you toss that one?"

"Because it was creepy."

"How?"

"It had bats and ghosts all over it. I don't like Halloween."

"Cause of the stuff some people do to hurt kids?"

"Do you need a better reason? The fun's been gone from Halloween for a long time. It's too much of a risk to be out asking strangers for candy. People don't know each other the way they used to. And, I can get candy at home and dress up as anything else *whenever I please*."

"*I wonder what makes someone want to poison kids?*"

"Maybe something bad was done to them; a bad trick. I don't know the causes but there *are* some people doing it. Maybe each has their special reason. Maybe they're just crazy! It's depressing," she says, soundin like a teacher. "Children shouldn't have to fear treats."

"Nia, are your pencils magic?"

She looks at me funny for a few seconds then giggles:

"Sho, if you want them to be!"

She gets up an runs over to clap hands an sing wit some a the girls. I get up an go play basketball.

Nex thing I know, most a the boys is jumpin rope. Nia got them to do it by talkin bout how boxers train.

Chapter 12

Terry

The following day in math class I'm tryin to watch The Collector's new efforts as much as I can. The teacher — Mr. Burns — calls me to his desk.

"Why are you staring at Terry so much, Malcolm? Don't you know that doesn't make the situation any better?"

"But Mr. Burns, The Col — I mean — Terry is actually doing some work!"

"I will admit he's doing something but I wouldn't call it work. He's goofed off too long to suddenly catch up. Now go sit down and complete *your* work. *And try minding your own business.*"

Sometimes I can't figure teachers out. To me, the fact that Terry is even *doin anything* should mean somethin. I guess Mr. Burns thinks if he pays too much attention it'd make Terry stop. But I think it's more like too-lil-too-late an not worth gettin excited over for teachers who act like "Mistuh Burns." I bet he don't even like kids.

When I bring the news to Ms. Winston she gives Terry some workbooks she'd been savin for just such a occasion. She even thanks me for tellin her. An Terry continues to work. It don't seem to bother him that he's doin diffrent work than the rest a us. He seems OK wit just doin somethin.

Ms. Marla Winston *got it*! She's one a the best an most carin teachers in the whole school. Mostly everybody in our class *really* like her. She's got us under control but it feels like we free anyway cuz we all know just how far to push her.

Ms. Winston is truly interested in everything "*her children*" think an do. I'd asked her was she married an did she have any kids. She said yes to both. That seems to be hard to do in my mind; work wit kids all day an come home to some too! But I guess since she can handle us, she probly don't have much trouble at home.

Becuzza her ways, Ms. Winston hardly ever hastuh send anybody to the office for serious misbehavin. She don't even need to use Mr. King that much. Kids that just act out be sent to him. He's famous for his bad breath, so we call him B. B. King but not to his face. I heard that somebody lef a bottle a mouthwash on his desk once! I don't think he took the hint. Mr. King's breath be *so bad* you do your work—an quietly—just so he don't come over to talk to you! It smells so rotten it hangs in the air after he walks away! Then you gotta check to see if your face melted! I know first-hand from when I was sent to him for laughin at a girl's hair cuz some a her fake braids was fallin out.

Anyway, it feels good when I please Ms. Winston. Just the look on her pretty face is enough. One time she took me an Nia out in the hall an tol us how special we was an that if there was anything she could do to help us develop our talents, to please let her know. She said we could write her a note cuz she didn't wanna hurt the other children's feelins but she didn't wanna neglect us either. She said:

"Now, I don't expect either of you to return to the classroom and share what I just told you. This is between the three of us and your parents."

For Ms. Winston to be straight up wit me an Nia like that was *real cool!*

It's nice to be noticed for bein good at things. In some classes, the teachers hardly got time to really get wit those tryin to learn cuzza the ones actin out. It'd be diffrent if we — who usely behave — could tune out the foolishness. But it's *real hard* not gettin involved or laughin cuz we got some *professional clowns* in class!

Chapter 13

Appreciation

J am's got some tickets for a jazz concert he an Mom was sposed to go to but she has to work late so she asks me if I'd like to go. I tell her sho but Jam better not try to kiss me good night! This time she laughs out loud!

"Well, you should have a good time. Even if you don't really like the music, I'm sure you'll be able to appreciate all the work that goes into it, right?"

"Yeah, Mom. Appreciation: finding worth in what is being presented, whether I understand it or not."

"I guess that's one way of looking at it. You *could* try to sound a little more excited. You and Jam haven't been out together for some time! Dress nice. Have fun for me!"

"*Yeah! OK! Thanks! Bye!*"

"Bye, young man."

Jam arrives round seven o'clock. We tell the other he looks good. It's kinda a joke we got goin whenever I go wit him someplace special. It means my mom would approve a us.

The performance is at fancy Orchestra Hall. I see there's three big name performers doin the concert together. I remember hearin somethin bout all a them.

Goin to music performances always makes me think a how much I wanna learn how to play the piano. "Hey Jam, could you teach a young brotha to play the *conga* drums?

"Probly. But you gotta have music in your *heart, mind an soul* if you really, *really* wanna play a instrument the way it's meant to be played. *Any* instrument."

I guess I lean toward the piano cuzza how masterful I feel usin a computer keyboard. But I realize I got more of a chance learnin from Jam.

I think a the time I enjoyed one a my dad's jazz records. I was alone at his crib an playin some ole vinyl that had belonged to his dad, my Granpa Richard, Sr. He'd passed five years before Dad came to America (Granma Lula still lives in Jamaica. She's due for a visit soon!). The record I played is by a African musician but it's more jazzier than I thought African music would be. I think it was by Hugh somebody.

Once we get to our seats, I ask Jam if he ever heard of a African jazz man named Hugh. He says right away:

"You *must* mean *Hugh Masekela.*"

"Yeah, that sounds right. So he's a big deal, huh?"

"Yes, a *very* big deal. He's been around for some time. You know about that movie *Sarafina?*"

"Yeah. I seen it."

"Well, Masekela wrote an performed some a the music for it. I can't remember if he was just playin the trumpet or the *flugel horn* cuz he plays so many instruments. But this isn't helpin you cuz you never saw the play, right?"

"Nope, never did."

"OK, OK. You ever heard a 'Grazing in the Grass'?"

"I think so."

"I'll play some a his music on the way back. I always got

that one in my car. It was his first big hit in the States back in the sixties!."

"OK." *Man*, Hugh *What's-his-name* gotta be a *serious big deal* to Jam! I settle in my seat an get ready to be appreciative.

When the first set is over, I'm actualy enjoyin myself! We got nice seats an every thing sounds so good like those movie theaters wit surround sound. You can almost separate each instrument an concentrate on it. Jam is pleased. He can tell I'm feelin the music. Soon as the musicians take a break, he tells me he's goin to the restroom.

"Stay here an keep an eye on my leather, ah'ight?"

"Sho, an I'll go when you get back."

"That's right. I won't take long."

The musicians is already returnin to the stage when I get back. I'm thinkin that they should have a singer. But now, the saxaphone is fillin that space. I even close my eyes while listenin. I think jazz is like everything thrown together but on purpose. Jam calls it *"gumbo for the ears."*

It's weird. Everytime I hang out wit Jam I learn somethin new. Just like wit my dad. Maybe that's one a the reasons Jam an Mom be together.

On the way home, I'm listenin to "Grazing in the Grass" — which I do remember hearin — an a few other cuts by Hugh. I'm once again enjoyin while appreciatin.

I'm one lucky dude to have somebody as cool as Jam wanna hang wit *me* on a Friday night — ha, ha.

Chapter 14

Game

My dad picks me up early on Saturday to go to the park, then we get Juan Lee an Kenyon. Dad has all the sports equipment we need in his trunk.

We start by throwin the soft ball an tryin to get one person out at a time before they reach home plate. Then we take turns goin up for bat an do the same thing. We throw long passes to each other wit the football — an as teams — try to intercept the passes.

Dad gets out the soccer ball an explains how to play to Kenyon an Juan Lee. Kenyo wants to know more bout the head buttin a the ball. Juan Lee says he knows he'll be good at soccer cuz he can kick the same rock all the way from home to wherever he's goin.

Dad explains:

"Kicking a soccer ball is the easy part once you develop the touch. But kicking while other feet are trying to take the ball from you is *much* different —"

"Hey, Dad," I interrup. "I know what Pele's real name is."

"OK, son. Let's hear it."

I make a funny face while I dig a piece a paper out a my pocket. "He's a great soccer player," I tell the others. "It's Edison Aran-tes do Nas-ci-men-to."

"No wonder they call him Pele." Kenyo smirks while wipin his glasses on his shirt.

Dad says:

"I don't know about the pronunciation but that's a hard name to remember. Do you know anything else about him?"

"Yeah." I look at my paper again. "He was born in 1940. His home team in Brazil won three world championships under his leadership in 1958, 1962 and 1970. He came out of retirement to play in the U.S. with the *New York Cosmos* during 1975 to '77." I bow after my readin an receive a small round a applause.

"Where'd you find all that out; on the 'net?" Juan Lee wonders.

"Naw, in that giant encyclopedia in the school library." I reply proudly. Dad playfully pops me on the head an says:

"OK, *showoff*, I'm impressed. Tell us some about David Beckham next time."

He continues explainin soccer:

"The main objective is to kick the ball to the goal. A player can use his head and chest too but we'll deal with that later. The only players who can touch the ball with their hands are the goalkeepers. OK?"

We all say *"yeah."*

"All right. Let's start with you moving the ball with your feet; use both of them," Dad orders.

We each take turns kickin the ball across the playfield.

"Good. Now, let's try it faster while keeping control of the ball. That's a little harder to do. Juan, kick the ball while Kenyon tries to take it ... OK, you see that makes it much harder, right?"

We nod. Juan Lee an Kenyon seem to be enjoyin theyselves.

"OK, Malcolm, you try kicking the ball while Kenyon *and* Juan try to get it from you."

Since I know how to manuever the ball pretty good, neither one is able to get it from me.

"Now, watch this." Dad grins.

He quickly an smoothly takes the ball from me wit just a lil foot action an more aggression.

"*That* is known as a *tackle*, my boys."

Dad gets Juan Lee an Kenyon to try to take it from me again. This time I havtuh really work to keep control. Then Kenyo tackles me. We play for a while wit Dad an Juan Lee on one team an me an Kenyo on the other. It's a lot more fun than just me an my father alone!

We work on tryin to lift the ball up to our chests an heads an tossin it to each other's teammate. We probly look like The Three Stooges! When it's time to rest, Dad gives each a us a bottle a water to sip an tells some more bout the game.

"A real game goes on for 45 minutes — breaks — an then goes for another 45 minutes. I'm not sure what the amount of time is for youth. I think it'd be a perfect game for you all to play but for some reason it hasn't caught on with many African American kids."

Juan Lee asks:

"Mr. B., can we play basketball?"

"Nope. You young folk need to learn how to play something other than basketball. Everybody *ain't* going to make it to the NBA."

I think bout the after school coach who almost did. I can tell my boys is thinkin the same thing.

Dad asks:

"How those ear plugs working out, Juan?"

"Oh, makin things better. Thanks Mr. B!"

"You're most welcome, son."

"Let's play some more soccer!" Kenyon shouts.

We practice a bit an then we play us three against Dad.

He shows no mercy; runnin up an down the field as if we ain even there. We play until we're really hot an tired out. I wanna take off my sweatshirt but it's got too cold for that. I think bout tennis, golf, an even hockey bein other sports to try.

"Man, we should add soccer to our game playin!" Juan Lee decides.

Then both boys speak together:

"Thanks Mr. Ba-kers-field an Wat-cher."

They say it together like singin. I give them a look that says *I caught that.*

As we leavin, I notice somebody sittin on the bench farther down the field. I keep lookin real hard cuz I think it might be Martin. Whoever it is don't wave or nothin, so I don't either.

The nex time I see Martin, I ask was he at the park while we was there. He says *"yeah."*

"Why didn'tchu wave or somethin, man?"

"Cuz I was meetin somebody an I didn't wanna get involved witchu jus then."

"That's cold, man. You could a at lease said *hey* to your peeps."

"An what if I did an then y'all come over to talk an invite me to hang witchu an stuff. Meanwhile, the person I'm waitin to see keeps goin."

"Ah'ight. Guess whatevuh you into was more important at the time."

"Yeah, part a how I makes my day. What I do ain nobody's bidness but mine."

"You sayin I would bust on you?" I ask, a lil offended.

"Naw, man. It's all on a need to know basis. An you — *nosy* — don't need to know."

"OK, brotha. I just wonder how you doin sometimes."

"I'm makin it. Jus a private person bout some things."

"So, you still readin a book a week, geek?"

"Man, *yeah*. I still wanna learn stuff, jus not in the local '*jail*'. Whenever I go there I take out some library books, hang out in a class or two, chat up my girl Patrice, an *book wit my books* — hah! At home, I watch a lotta public TV an cable shows that teach history an stuff. I can always go to the public library for whatever else I wanna read."

"I thought Patrice gave up on you. You got a library card, man?"

"Yeah, an *so*?"

"That's cool. You still plannin to go to school after you sixteen?"

"I don't know, man. I'm so bored when I'm there. I don't know. I been thinkin bout taking the GED.

"You will if you drop out, right?"

"Yeah, OK. Anything new goin on witchu an Mom?"

"Not really. Everything's cool."

"How's Granma Sil doin? I been thinkin bout her cuz it's near the date Granpa Sil passed. Two years ago, right?"

"Yeah. She's doin good. She asked bout you. Oh, yeah. I wrote Unc Walter."

"That's good. I need to do that too. Imagine what he must be dealin wit! Call me an gimme his address. I can't find it at the house. Hey, you got a girl yet? I saw you wit one."

"When?"

"Yeah, I saw you a few days back. Talkin to that cutie wit the locks at a bus stop."

"That's a girl from my class. She's super smart an I can talk to her bout anything. She's the most interestin person I've met in a *long* time. Almost as interestin as my big brotha. Maybe more cuz she don't mind tellin me what she's up to."

I thought bout all the secrets Martin thinks he's hidin from me. Like — for instance — he got a cell phone.

"Ya'll billin an cooin yet?" He flicks the toothpick he was chewin on out into the street.

"*We ain birds*! But naw, we just close. Have a lotta stuff in common. I guess I'd like her to be but it ain like that wit us. She's more like a best friend." After I say that, I look at Martin *real serious* an tell him: "Now don't be teasin me. . ."

Martin laughs.

"I ain gon tease you. You jus ain really into the females yet an this the first one I ever seen you spend time wit."

"Whatchu doin? Flyin around in a helicopter or somethin?"

"I'm jus keepin track a my lil bro is all. Wanna know you OK."

"It's just the same for me, Martin." I'm feelin all emotional now, which I hate. If we wasn't on the street I'd make Martin hug me. For now, we just grab hands an bump shoulders.

"We'll get together an do somethin soon, OK?"

I nod an head home.

Chapter 15

New Assignment

For social studies we havtuh do research an a report on somethin we're interested in. I'm tryin to decide if I wanna write bout soccer or racin. I decide to pick racin cuz I know so much bout it. An, I still got the info I found while lookin up Willy T. Ribbs. My moms is right. I can use what I'd saved to do my paper. I'd already printed out most a what I'd need. I ask Nia what she's gonna report on.

"*Ancient Egypt!*"

She tries to stand the way they drew theyselves back then. I have to laugh cuz she looks so clumsy! Then she says:

"Mayhaps I'll write about Mr. Barack Obama instead. He might be our next president, you know."

"I figure a lot a kids'll be doin that. *I've* decided to write about the manly art of motor sports," Nia has her mouth open to tell me something else but I beat her to it. "I *know* there's women racers but my report is gonna be on African American racers an I ain seen nothin on no black female drivers." I find my printouts an notes on racin an try to school Juan Lee durin Brainstorming Time in class. We got a week to do our reports an I figure he'll need help. Juan Lee decides to write bout break dancin cuz he's so into it. I start tellin him some a what I'll use for my report. I play it like I'm givin a lecture so he'll laugh.

"First African American driver I learned about was one my father told me of by the name of Willy T. Ribbs." Juan Lee starts chucklin an says:

"Is that *really* his name?"

"Yes, young man, *it tis.* As I was saying, I learned from many sites on the Internet that he raced for almost 25 years and was the most *win-nin-gest* African American driver in history! He won Driver of the Year twice and was the first black man to compete in NASCAR's Winston Cup Series. Mr. Ribbs — for a long time — had been the first, and only, African American to test for the Formula One Grand Prix team in Portugal! He retired from racing and took up clay shooting because he had trouble getting enough sponsors. Advertising for their sponsors are the reason drivers and their cars have so many patches, painted words and symbols on them.

Hungry for more information, I put in a search for black racing car drivers. I found one site that mentions a Mr. Wendell Scott who was the first African American stock-car driver. He won the Grand Nationals in 1963!

There is also Mr. Morty Buckles who raced in the Indianapolis Motor Speedway in 2002. And, I discovered, on The American Racing Car Association site, a Mr. Herbert Bagwell, Jr., also known as The Hawk. He and his wife own and operate Bagwell Motor Sports. In an interview, Mr. Bagwell stated he could use a lot more sponsors and would like to see more black folk racing and watching in the stands.

And there's Mr. Leonard Miller, co-owner of The Miller Racing Group. He was the first black owner in the Indianapolis 500! He wrote a book, Silent Thunder, that tells about his experiences in the business of racing.

As far back as the 1920's there existed a heartland racing sweepstakes called The Gold and the Glory, formed by blacks because they weren't allowed to compete in the Indy

500. You can compare them to The Negro Leagues of baseball that were also formed due to exclusion.

And, most recently, there's a Mr. Lewis Hamilton whom I need to research further. Mr. Lee, *are you taking all this down?*" Juan Lee busts out laughin. He enjoyed my lil presentation an he wasn't the only one. Nia is smilin an softly clappin her hands.

Juan Lee — still laughin — says:

"Watcher, *you crazy*! But seriously, man, you gonna havtuh help me out wit my paper. I don't think I'll be able to find much bout *breakin, krumpin an steppin* in books."

"Not a problem, my brotha." I smile.

"Brainstorming Time is over, class." Ms. Winston announces.

I strut my way back to my seat.

Chapter 16

Sports Center

True to his word, Martin called on Friday night to see what was up for tomorrow. I tol him not too much. He said *"cool"* an that he'd meet me at four. I clear it wit Mom.

When Martin arrives, he hugs an kisses Mom as usual.

"You're going to the sports center, right? What time do you plan to be back?."

"Bout nine."

"That's a bit late to be on the bus. What if I pick you two up instead?"

"That'd be cool." Martin agrees.

We leave an walk over to Ole Jess' house. Jess is home as usual. Soon as we inside, Martin picks up the phone an calls a cab to Jess' address. I guess I'm lookin a lil skeptical cuz Martin says:

"What? We takin a cab, is all! Jess, you gon have those papers for me tonight?"

"Sho will, *Mr. Davis!*"

Martin must be talkin bout all the slips a paper spread

out on Jess' card table. I wonder what they for. An there's a new lookin computer on a desk an a backpack layin nearby. Why'd Jess need those? Somethin tells me not to ask.

The taxi arrives an we say "*later*" to Jess. Martin tells the driver to take us to Wonderworld Sports Center. I ask Martin bout the computer. I figure he can handle that question now.

"It's *mine*, oh inquisitive one! Jess is keepin it for me cuz it'll be safer there."

"That's the same reason we got your *other* one at the house."

"I lef it there for you, Malc. An for Mom. I got the other at Jess' cuz I can use it *anytime*, like two o'clock in the a.m. I got a key to his house. Occasionally I sleep there — since you need to know so much. Mistuh Eddie '*Playa*' Davis ain that easy to play — or live wit — even though he hardly ever around. Sometimes he don't want me there for what seems like no reason at all. I havtuh call before I come home if it's after nine. I don't think he'd miss me if I stayed away for a *month*."

I almost ask Martin what else his dad be doin to him but I hold back.

We ride the go-carts first an have so much fun we hardly do anything else. We play miniature golf an I do a lil better than Martin — I think he let me. We have Coney dogs, chili fries, an pop; *real junk food!* We talk bout whatever comes up. I think to myself that Martin still knows what I like. He reminds me that this is his treat an won't let me spend money for *nothin*.

Too soon it's time for us to meet Mom at the entrance. She's bout ten minutes late so we mess wit her for that. We laugh bout what we made the go-carts do until Mom stops at Martin's house.

He climbs out a the back seat, bows low an says:

"Thanks *milady*. I'll be in touch," like he a superhero or somethin. He lopes on up the steps, takes out his keys an stands by the door. He waves *bye* wit a lotta exaggeration til we pull off. I figure this is all a show for Mom. Martin'll pro-bly wait five minutes an hit the streets again.

I hope he ain involved in nothin dangerous.

Chapter 17

You Did It

Ms. Quayle — the school sub — asks Nia to sharpen 32 new pencils; one for each a us. She's tired a kids goin to the sharpener or beggin for pencils. She ain really fooled, though, cuz she says she'll make sure the reglar teacher knows bout it. She also collects our ole pencils an puts them in the Freebie Can. Even The Collector gives one up.

Now, I figure this'll *prove* that Nia's touch is magic.

I watch. The class is startin to act out cuz Mr. Sanchez — who usely teaches us at this time — ain in the room. But as soon as they get they spankin new pencil — all a them *get busy wit the work!* It's almost as if Mr. Sanchez is at the controls. Ms. Quayle looks real happy cuz she thinks we just bein good an she ain gonna havtuh punish us, send anybody to B.B. or the office.

One a the security guards — Mr. Colquitt — peeks in an keeps a-steppin. Everybody is *on task*. Ms. Quayle is walkin up an down the rows, answerin questions an helpin some students get unstuck. I can tell she's enjoyin bein able to *actualy teach!* Mr. Sanchez lef two worksheets for us to do an a word search puzzle for those who finish the assignments. All three is in Spanish. Ms. Quayle is explainin an passin out one assignment every ten minutes.

I'm enjoyin the peacefulness in the room cuz we also hav-tuh work on makin sentences out a all our new spellin words for Ms. Winston. I really like doin that cuz I let my imagi-nation *go crazy!* Sometimes I turn all the words into a story. There usely be one to them. You just havtuh think bout how they relate. Since I ain as good at blockin noise like Nia, the class bein quiet is just what I need.

When Mr. Sanchez returns from his prep, he fusses some bout us buggin Ms. Quayle into givin us new pencils. I volun-teer a challenge: "How about a contest, Mr. Sanchez? Whoever makes their new pencil last for seven school days'll get a *prize!*"

"Good idea, Malcolm!"

Nia an I ain in the contest cuz I was already makin mine last an she needs two pencils every week, even though she brings her own. Mr. Sanchez gets out a bottle a some weird color nail polish he'd confiscated. He paints it on the pen-cils — right above the erasers — for ID.

The nex week, Mr. Sanchez hastuh hand out thirty-two bags a chips as prizes. He'd decided to treat me an Nia too.

Nia looks at me toward the end a the day an I whisper three words to her: "*You did it.*" She giggles an shakes her head *no*; her hair bouncin like soft rope. I get into her face an repeat "You did it! You did it!" I'm determined to make her own up to her powers. An she's just as determined not to admit to anything.

She laughs:

"You quit it! You quit it!"

"Admit it! Admit it!"

Nia just laughs as if darin me to say somethin else. I would if I could think a another rhyme at the time. Nobody's payin any attention to us. Too busy munchin they chips. I think to myself: *There's much more for you to know — once you've seen a pencil glow.*

When we get back to homeroom for dismissal, Ms. Winston is pleased there ain no bad behavior notes from Mr. Sanchez for the second week in a row.

I wonder how many'll still have the same pencil nex week. But it don't matter cuz Ms. Winston puts Nia in charge a sharpenin pencils. She claims it's cuz she bought a new electric sharpener but I'm guessin she's beginnin to *see the light* — ha, ha.

Chapter 18

Trouble

On Friday, Lakita Pugh — a tall bully in Kenyo's class — comes out angry onto the playground. She has to fight a lot just cuz her mom is white. Kids always messin wit her for that an her last name. Some call her "P. U." Lakita gives out a lotta butt-whippins just to prove she ain no diffrent from nobody else an not afraid, neither. An she's used to bein the only girl gettin the best grades in *every* class. So today, she fronts Nia.

"An who do you think you are? You *'Little Miss Perfect of Gillespie School,'* right?"

"No, I'm Nia Stellar."

Lakita wasn't expectin that so she hastuh think a somethin else to say. She looks Nia up an down cuz she wants to fight. Nia says:

"I'm sort've new here. Who're you?"

They never spoke to each other before this. Lakita usely plays b-ball wit the boys or reads one a her paperbacks.

"I'm the one who's goin to kick yo behind, that's who!"

"Why?" Nia shrugs; her palms up.

"Becuz you makin me look bad," Lakita snarls.

"You seem to be making that happen all by yourself."

Lakita cusses Nia an swings at her but Nia ducks just in

time. Lakita tries again an the same thing happens. Just as I'm bout to break it up, Nia, speakin in a diffrent tone, tells Lakita:

"Stop wasting your time on unnecessary fear. Be the best you can be."

Lakita freezes like a statue then stalks off, still angry. Minutes later, it's like none of it happened. The girls who are jumpin rope continue as Lakita an Nia join them. I'm the only one who seems to have witnessed the almost fight. I ask Juan Lee an Kenyon:

"Did y'all see that?"

"See what?" Kenyon asks.

"Yeah, whatchu talkin bout, Watcher? *You always seein or hearin somethin!*" Juan Lee grumbles.

I'm feelin super-silly now, "Two girls almost got into a fight. *Y'all didn't see that?*"

"Nope," Juan Lee says. Kenyo slowly shakes his head at me as if I'm losin it. Both go back to shootin hoops.

I'm lookin real puzzled at Nia. She's still jumpin rope but turns to look at me as if to say: *Yes, we almost had a fight but I stopped it. You didn't imagine it.*

One a these days she's goin to admit her powers to me cuz I can't take much more a her pretendin I don't know. I look away, pick up a jump rope an imagine I'm Muhammad Ali.

Chapter 19

Truth

The nex time I see Martin, he's walkin toward his dad's. Jus as I'm bout to call him — a neighbor — Mr. Mason, comes out a his house in his pajamas an robe. He slowly jogs up to Martin — who meets him halfway — an gives him some pieces a paper. Martin looks them over an pushes them into his pocket as they wave *bye* to each other. I catch up to Martin, say *"hey,"* an ask him what he's doin.

"What do you mean what am I doing? Minding my business, as usual."

I decide it was now or never an say, "Martin, you a numbers runner ainchu?"

"And who are you, the *FBI?*"

"Naw, man. I'm just real observant. Runs in the famly, you know."

Martin shoots me a look that could cut metal. "Look, man, I'm sorry to be all up in your bizness an stuff but how long didchu think it would take me to figure it out? I see them pieces a paper most every place I see you. I bet Mom an Auntie Evelyn know bout it. Shoot, much as olduh people like to play, Granma Sil may too."

"You finished?"

"I guess."

"First of all, this is one of those things you don't *need* to know. However, you make a good point. Since you're part of the neighborhood and growing up and all, it was a wonder you didn't know sooner. I just keep thinking of you as my *younger brother*, you know? I'm sorry that you're probably *really* disappointed in me right now but you'll get over it. I'll stop when I'm ready to and you have to respect that."

"Do I have a choice?"

"Not really. We're still brothers but I gotta do what I gotta do."

"But that's the thing! You ain gotta do it!"

"Look, Malcolm, I have never been perfect and I have never tried to be. Running numbers is only a *misdemeanor* and I'm considered a *minor*, you know. I don't plan to keep doing it much longer. I don't have a record and I'm not trying to get one. You be you and I be me. And we agree to disagree."

"Martin, I just don't wanna see you in trouble. A misdemeanor can still get you locked up. You already known as truant an violatin curfew. You wanna be known as a *juvenile delinquent*? That's all I'm gonna say." I know his patience won't last much longer cuz he's talkin standard E. *"The calm before the storm,"* my mother calls it. I take a chance an say one more thing: "You my brotha an I love you but I don't havtuh like what you're doin."

"That's exactly right."

We go our separate ways.

Chapter 20

Poetry an Monsters

For homeroom today, we all sposed to have a poem bout Halloween. I brought two poems that Martin wrote wit my mother — before she really started to hate Halloween — bout five years ago. Ms. Winston calls on me to begin. "These two poems have been in our family for years.

'A Pumpkin Can Look Mean

I don't care much for pumpkin meat
But I do love the seeds.
I like to squish the stuff inside
It feels like old wet weeds.
I like the way a pumpkin feels
All smoothy roughy clean.
But most of all
I like the way
A
Pumpkin
Can
Look
Mean!

A Different Story

Black cat crossed my path today,
I didn't even care.
Gonna take much more'n that,
To give ME a scare!
Rattling bones, creaks and groans,
May make your flesh quiver,
Just look at me — I guarantee,
You won't even see a shiver.
But October 31st, on October 31st,
Now that's a different story!
When ghosts and bats, witches and cats,
Are all in their glory!
Jack-o-lanterns, vampires,
These things are seldom seen,
Except on October 31st,
When things are HALLOWEEN!"'

Everyone claps for both poems. My mother says she's gonna make a poetry book for all the holiday seasons one day. I wonder if Martin would be mad if he knew I'd read the poems.

It turns out that a lotta kids brought the poem, "Skeleton Parade," by Jack Pre-lut-sky. It's one a my favorites too. The teacher chooses Juan Lee to read it.

When he finishes, we all clap for Juan Lee. He'd really put a lotta expression into his readin. Reminds me a playin Monster in the Haystack! Maybe I can get some kids to play it durin lunchtime! More kids read diffrent poems an we all listen an applaud. Ms. Winston had allowed Nia to recite one bout fall. Then she asks for volunteers to read poems to the pre-school kids on up to the second graders right before lunch. I raise my hand while watchin Nia. She don't even turn around when I'm picked.

"Now," Ms. Winston announces, "It's everyone's turn to create a poem of their own."

She draws a big pumpkin on the board an puts some words we suggest inside it. After we write our poems, we copy them over — as neat as we can — an attach them to the paper pumpkins hangin outside the room. I *always* keep the first draft a my poems cuz I got a notebook to put them in. You never know.

Later, on the playground, I get Kenyo, Juan Lee an Lakita to play Monster in the Haystack. At first Nia don't wanna play but after watchin for a while she joins in.

Some other kids come over an we really have a good time! Most kids get so good at the game they get to be the monster more'n once! I never thought've it as a Halloween type thing before. *Just imagine the monster wearin a real mask!*

Chapter 21

Halloween

Halloween is tomorrow an only the pre-school kids an kindergardeners would be allowed to wear they costumes to school. All week the kids in our class been bringin in treats for our party. Nia brought cups an napkins for everybody. Ms.Winston would bring the drinks.

While we quietly doin our readin assignment, Ms. Winston says:

"Class, I have an announcement to make."

We all wait.

"Except for twelve people, everyone got an *A* or a *B* on their social studies reports! And those twelve people got *C's*! We are going to have to celebrate in a big way tomorrow because this is really something! Most of the people who usually got *B's* got *A's*! Those who usually get *C's* got *B's* and those who usually get *D's* got *C's*! *Very impressive!* Keep it going!"

I try to catch Nia's attention but she's busy talkin wit other kids.

The followin day is goin pretty much the same, we keepin the noise down in all our classes an tryin otherwise to be good.

Nobody wants to miss out on the party cept maybe Nia. Yesterday we had some art time for makin things to decorate our room. Nia made a drawin a pumpkins in the moonlight. That's as close as she'd go to get up for the day.

At party time each kid passes out what they brought. Ms. Winston is lettin us listen to some audiotapes an CD's she'd pre-approved.

I notice Nia ain gettin as many treats as everybody else. I ask her why an she says she's only takin ones witout Halloween stuff on them. She's bein polite bout it but some kids is wonderin why she ain takin some that's offered to her. They could understand if she was a *Jehovah's Witness* or somethin.

"Besides," she tells me, "I'm going to help with the pre-school and kindergarten class parties. I'll get some treats there too."

I tell her that she should be lettin the others know so they don't get wrong ideas bout why she's refusin some treats. But she don't think it's necessary. I guess I'm bein a pest but I havtuh ask her one last question: "Nia, did somethin bad happen to you on Halloween?"

"No. I just don't like it; remember? I like 'Ancestor's Night.' It's sort of like Halloween but you dress as cultural heroes like African kings and queens and other famous black people from the past. There's a program and food to sample, games to play and maybe a visit to other places."

"Is that what you're gonna do tonight?"

"No. I don't know of any place that does it here. I don't think my parents do, either."

"What if I find a place? My mother's boyfriend probly knows somewhere we can go."

"Oh, that'd be *great!*"

When I get out a school I jog straight to my mama's job. I

ask her, "Ma, does Jam know about some place where people celebrate African stuff instead of Halloween?"

"I'm sure he does. Why are you asking me that, sweetheart?"

"My friend from class wants to go to a place where it's done. Could you call Jam and ask him, please?"

My mother looks me over an says: "This must be really important for you to get all mannerly. Hold on, I'll call him — Hi Honey, Malcolm wants to go to a party where people celebrate African culture on Halloween."

"You talkin bout 'Ancestor's Night,' baby?"

I can hear his voice boomin from the phone. I bob my head up an down.

"Yeah, that sounds like it," Mom says, "Where do they have it around here?"

"At The Nubian Club. The owners make the club look as much like an African village as possible an children can come an celebrate up to nine p.m."

"You know I don't get off work until eight, right? Do you think you could take Malcolm and his friend? I can pick them up."

"*No prob!* I meant to tell you I'm playin there tonight. Let Malc know I'll meet him at the house at six-thirty. Tell him to dress like a *positive* ancestor but if he can't, it's no big deal. He'll still be welcome. An *I* will bring them home. You just enjoy bein alone for a minute."

"Thank you, honey."

"*Always a pleasure, baby!*"

"Thanks Mom!" I shout, an run home to call Nia.

Chapter 22

Ancestors' Night

L ater we meet Nia at the club. She'd been waitin in the car wit her mother. Jam an me introduce ourselves to Ms. Stellar an I try to be charmin. Jam tells Ms. Stellar we can take Nia home after the party. They exchange cell phone numbers an Ms. Stellar drives off.

Jam grins at us an says: "I like your costumes, *watotos*! I'm sure you two will enjoy yourselves. As for me, I'll be entertainin you with my African drums tonight!" After introducin us to a few a the folks in charge, he goes to talk to the other performers.

Nia an me had done our best to look like famous ancestors. I'm Frederick Douglass wit an ole suit a Martin's an my hair parted mostly to one side an slicked down. I 'd made a beard out a painted cotton balls. Nia's Harriet Tubman. She's got on a long dress an ole boots an a scarf on her head.

She says:

"Who had a greater purpose than she?"

I agree. I notice a girl in a big tee shirt wit a large, capital N, in the middle of a tombstone on it. Must have somethin to do wit the ole "N Word."

When it's time to eat, we try mango, smoked fish, fresh coconut, *jollof* rice, spicy chicken wit some kinda greens, goat meat stew, peanut soup, boiled peanuts, *injera* bread, an fried *plantain* (I always wondered what those big, green bananas was for!). After eatin, we play cultural type games like *mancala* an dominoes. Then it's time for us to give lil speeches. When it's my turn, I say:

"Slavery was a horrible thing for our people to exist under. We were treated worse than mules. I was determined to be free. I secured my own freedom by escaping to the North and taught myself to read so I could speak honestly and clearly to my people about this *peculiar institution* which allowed persons to have ownership over other human beings."

Nia's turn is nex. She makes her voice go deep an tells bout how hard life was for the enslaved people:

"Ah was hit in the head as a chile by the massa an Ah still suffers *spells*. But Ah could not live as a slave! After Ah freed myself, Ah went back to the South at lease nineteen times to help othas to escape. As a conductor, Ah led ovuh 300 of our people to freedom through The Underground Railroad. *An-Ah-nevuh-lost-a-passenger.*"

I get chills after Nia says that.

Last, it was the turn a the girl wit the big N on her shirt. She begins:

"I am the tomb of the N Word. I have been taught by my ancestors and elders to never allow the word *nigger* to fly from my mouth. Here, I am talking about its ugliness, so I have allowed myself to speak it. As you all know, people have died physically and mentally over this word. Yet today, we hear it repeatedly from those who don't realize that it too is dead. If you proudly parade the word and continue to breathe life into it, you cannot speak sincerely against its use and how — and by whom — it is used. You're giving permission to do so without remorse or understanding! This word can never be *just a word*. Saying it over and over will not remove its sting from our deepest memories. The N Word is *dead*. Let us hold its funeral everyday. *Let our pride be revived!*" She ends by holdin up a fist an turnin slowly witin the circle so we all can see her shirt. There is loud applause from everybody! I wonder how she could remember all a that speech. That girl really gave me a lot to think bout!

The audience claps again for all us children who made a speech, dressed specialy, an are just there. We also have a ceremony where we call upon our ancestors to help us in our need to remember who we are an where we come from. One a the kids begins to recite The Seven Principles by heart. Nia whispers to me:

"In *Kiswahili* it's called the *Nguzo Saba* from *Kwanzaa* celebration but you're supposed to practice the principles all year."

She recites along wit the kid as some others do. The fifth principle is called *nia*. It means purpose, I remember. I smile at my friend. When the program is done, it's back to playtime! We meet a lotta kids, some wit locks like Nia's. I don't see nobody else I know cept Jam. I introduce Nia an me to the girl wit the N Word shirt. She smiles and says:

"I'm Luna. I'm the goddess of the moon! Oh, excuse me! I always tell what my name means because people usually ask."

I keep lookin at Luna. Watchin her is like seein a pot boil over! She seems ready to take off into the sky! Her almost black eyes are dancin in her dark face. She never stops wavin her arms at her sides. "Well, we just wanted to meet you." I smile. I already knew her name had somethin to do wit the moon soon as she said it. Nia probly did too.

Nia tells her:

"Your speech was wonderful! And Luna is a lovely name!"

Luna is a lovely girl, I'm thinkin.

The musicians begin playin African music. I watch Jam an feel proud to know him. I ain heard much *"roots music"* — as he calls it — before but I was bobbin my head an pattin my feet. Nia's doin a lil back an forth rock. Luna an some other kids jump in front a the musicians an seem to be waitin for somethin.

Suddenly, some dancers in African clothes appear an give us a super fast lesson in how to dance to the music! Nia an me get pulled into the center — along wit the other boys an girls — an we all dance as African as we can! It's thrillin an *deep!* People makin shrieks an a sound like *lululululululu,* an clappin an shoutin. It feels like the drummin is my heartbeat. All the kids is lovin it. No one feels shame. I'm glad Mom got Jam to bring us.

When I tell him, he says:

"Anytime, young brotha!"

We press our knuckles together. Jam's golden face is smilin from ear to ear. He's always real happy when he's entertainin.

I ain never felt the way this night is makin me feel. The closest thing to it for me is in church when the pastor gets everybody to be free to talk out, move, an to feel the *Spirit.* I know somehow these things is connected.

When it's time to go, each a us gets a copy a the "Black Family Pledge" by Dr. Maya Angelou an the "Nguzo Saba" by Dr. Maulana Karenga. We also get to choose one a the games we'd played an get a bag a treats to take wit us.

Jam an me take Nia home. *Maaan,* she lives far from my neighborhood! No wonder her mom brings her to school everyday.

Nia bounces out a the car an says:

"Thank you for inviting me. Wait til it's time for the Kwanzaa celebrations!"

I'm glad I know somethin bout them already. I wonder

what Nia's family does for Thanksgiving an Christmas. On the way home I ask Jam if he'd perform at Gillespie on the last day before the holidays, when we have our Christmas Program.

"Yeah, I could do that. I'd be helpin make Kwanzaa more special, right?

"Right!"

My mother is pleased wit my costume. Jam tells her how intelligent an pretty Nia is an what a good job we did on our speeches. I get a lil shy bout it an go into my bedroom. I can tell they laughin at me but I don't care. I tape the papers on my wall, nex to Nia's drawin, an get into bed.

Man! I still hear them drums an cowbells an stuff while I'm fallin off to sleep.

Chapter 23

Science

C uz I stayed up late in order to go to Ancestors' Night it was a lil harder for me to wake up. I hadtuh run to catch up to Juan Lee. He's got a reliable alarm clock cuz he can't count on his parents to wake him. I got one too cuz I like to wake myself up on school days. Sorta like goin to my job.

I tell Juan Lee all bout my experiences at the nightclub an he says he would plan to go nex year.

"Are you Nia's boyfriend now?"

"No," I say quickly. "I just really like her."

"I like her too. She's not bossy or borin or all up in your face like some a the other girls."

"You know." I agree. We talk bout how some a the boys like girls to act like that.

Suddenly, we see two much older bigger boys walkin straight toward us. *Please don't let us havtuh fight* I say to myself. I'm just feelin better when they pass us by til one a them growls:

"Don'tchu lil school boys know how to speak?"

Both Juan Lee an I turn around an say together: "What up?"

"That's more like it. *You guys have a peachy-keen day now!*" Then they both laugh an walk away.

"They jus wanted to make us *sweat!*"

Juan Lee says angrily, his face red. He cusses an talks bout what he'd like to do to them boys. I try to relax myself an answer, "At lease they didn't touch us." I *really* hate the way it feels when you think you gotta fight. Your whole body gets ready an that feelin takes even longer to go away if the fight don't happen.

We make it to school witout any more incidents but still feelin a lil angry. Juan Lee is steady cussin. I wonder if those boys know whose brotha they was messin wit. I know Martin can't be everywhere I'm at but those boys could a beat us down an taken anything they wanted. That's why we let any girls we meet on the way walk to school wit us if they want. They usely got more to worry bout. "Just another day in the hood." I mumble. By the time Juan Lee an me reach the classroom, we're cool.

We got science class right after homeroom attendance is taken. I really like science but most a the class don't so somebody's always gettin in trouble. The teacher — Ms. Westbrooks — ignores what she can. She's determined not to let any lil thing disrup her teachin. But when some a the kids really act up — it affects the whole class. Then we end up doin more readin an writin assignments than experiments. Ms. Westbrooks tol us at the beginnin a the school year she didn't wanna send anybody out a the room unless it was *absolutely necessary.*

Today she reminds us that it's never too early to start thinkin bout projects for the Science Fair. Most everybody groans.

There's a way to learn more excitin things when not in

science class an that's by joinin the Science Club. Me an Nia belong an so do Kenyon an Lakita. Juan Lee ain all that interested. Besides, his grades ain good enough yet an we get to leave out a class in order to participate. We also allowed to eat lunch in the classroom when Ms. Westbrooks is there. She's a vegetarian an don't eat *no kind* a meat!

My favorite things is wrapped up in science. We got animals: a painted turtle, a frog, mice, a snake, an a rabbit in the classroom. We learn bout planets an how discoveries are made. I also enjoy lookin at stuff through the microscope. Learnin how things work is cool too.

Ms. Westbrooks really knows her subject so it's excitin to have her all to ourselves durin club time. Only twelve kids belong an we meet once a week. This is the time we feed the animals an learn more bout them. It's fascinatin to watch the snake squeeze a mouse an swallow it but kinda scary too. I'm amazed at Nia cuz *she* feeds the snake once in a while! A *girl* handlin a mouse an allowin a snake to take it from her! Lakita won't even watch him eat! Nia hastuh wash her hands first just to be sure there ain any food smell that might cause Caesar — a ball python — to mistake her hand for what he's sposed to snatch an constrict. Ms. Westbrooks says it's best to hold the mouse by its tail an let the snake take it cuz the mouse might hurt the snake in such a small space as his tank. She also explained that it'd be cruel to have the mouse frightened longer than necessary. She had tol the class:

"There are many ways nature can seem harsh."

An she would always ask us:

"Have any of you children become vegetarians yet?"

So far, we've all answered *"no."*

"Case closed!" she'd smile.

But I notice she keeps the mouse an rabbit's cages as far away from the snake as possible. I shiver to think that Caesar would one day be big enough to swallow the rabbit. Ms. West-brooks said before that time he'd be livin at the zoo.

We help clean the tanks an cages an get to handle all the animals before they eat. We even have races between the frog, rabbit an turtle. Frawg an Br'er Rabbit hop all over the place so *Señor Tortuga — Español* for Mr. Turtle — usely wins cuz it's easier keepin him in a straight line.

We get to talk bout astronomy or anything else we want. I always think bout my mom's promise to get me a telescope. I wanna know more about the *astro-chem-i-stry* a space! I *love* to learn all bout stars and stuff!

Sometimes I wonder why out a two sixth grade classes, there's so few a us in Science Club. But then, I'm glad too cuz we got lots a time for each a us to do somethin witout too much silliness goin on.

To me, science is learnin all bout life.

Chapter 24

Basketball

Me, Juan Lee an Kenyo finely make up our minds to join the after school basketball program. All we hadtuh do was get permission slips signed by our parents an show up wit gym shoes, tee shirts, shorts an a towel.

It's a one hour program that meets twice a week — Wednesdays an Fridays. Our first day we bein drilled on the basics like dribblin, guardin an stuff. We ain allowed to just play. This is kinda hard to take cuz it's sorta like bein in gym class wit no free time.

Three coaches run the program: Mr Wayne — the gym teacher, Mr. Thornton — who volunteers durin school hours, an Mr. Pruitt, who's the lead coach. He's the one who almost made it to the NBA. He hastuh be at lease six-seven!

They start us off wit five slow laps round the gym. Then we do some warm-up exercises. Later, we doin sit-ups, push-ups, an tug-o-war. We form two lines for a relay where we havtuh dribble an make two lay-up baskets before the nex person in our line can try. We also practice throwin an bouncin basketballs to each other from a distance.

The coaches put us in small groups so they can get an idea a who is best at what. We do get to play a real game wit each other but the coaches is still continuin to observe us. They puttin us in an takin us out in what seems to be no special order or team. I ask a teammate, James: "Was it much diffrent when ya'll first started?"

"Not too much but we sposed to be playin games wit other teams soon."

Me, Juan Lee an Kenyon is glad to hear that! I count sixteen a us. I ask James, "How many turned out at first?"

"About 25. Some was tol to leave due to attitude problems an some just dropped out."

After we done wit more drills, we have a cool down period where we do some stretchin an walkin round the gym. The coaches talk to us bout what we did well or need to do better.

Coach Wayne asks for any newcomers to raise they hands. Only five go up, includin mine, Kenyon's an Juan Lee's. We're given papers explainin the basics a basketball an the rules for the program.

Coaches Wayne an Pruitt thank everybody for comin an have us thank Coach Thornton for bein here now an durin school hours. We change back into our street clothes an leave.

"Is *that* it?" Kenyon whines.

But by the nex week, we all feelin muscle aches in places we didn't know could hurt. Guess the coaches know what they doin after all.

Chapter 25

Knowledge Is Power

I agree to meet Nia at the public library near me on Saturday. I hate to admit it but I ain been in there for some time. When I need to know somethin, I use the school library or the Internet — even though you can't believe everything you find on it. Nia does too but she loves bein round a lotta books.

We go right into the adult section. Nia's got permission to check out books from it as long as they not *inappropriate*. She shows me books on art, animation, African American history, racin cars, soccer, an whatever else I'm interested in. What's amazin is I can read an understand most a the words in the books.

Nia asks:

"Do you read newspapers?"

"Sometimes the comics."

"The reason I ask is because most articles are written so a person with an eighth grade education can read them."

"So if I can read some a the same books you read, that means I can read as if I'm in the eighth grade?"

"Most likely but you need to understand what you read also."

"Yeah, comprehension. But I can use a dictionary an learn new words that way."

We look at other books an I decide I havtuh renew my

library card. Nia chooses two books: one on Native American art an the other on fashion design. She checks them out an we leave to get some lunch. We can only afford the sub sandwich place on the corner — but we good company for each other, so it seems like a fancy restaurant.

After we finish, I walk Nia to her bus stop an talk wit her until the bus comes. Then I jog home.

At home, I pull out the entertainment an sports sections a the newspaper an begin to read. Just like at the library, I can read an understand most a it. I get my dictionary an feel like I'm part a some scientific discovery. I even have a discussion wit my mother regardin some a what I read. She's glad to see me takin an interest in readin the paper. I tell her she hastuh take me to renew my library card.

"I need to get mine renewed too Malcolm. And we could do that next Saturday. That would also be a good day to invite Nia over for dinner if you'd like. Oh, I've got something for you."

It's a letter from Uncle Walter! I carefully open it an read:

Dear Malcolm,

   I was glad to get your letter, nephew! It really made my day!

   I'm happy you're doing so well in school and that you have a "nice, new friend." I actually know a couple of the guys I'm stationed with from before. And I've made some new friends too. We are hanging in but there's not much to tell you about what we do. It's mostly repair work, waiting and looking out for each other.

Tell your mom I'll write her again soon.

Keep the letters coming!

Love,
Uncle Walter

Chapter 26

Dinner an War

At school, when I tell Nia my mother wants her to come over for dinner this Saturday, she responds:

"What about you? Do you want me to come to dinner too?"

"*Of course!*" Why does she havtuh tease me so much? In that way, she's just like the other girls! I ask her is there anything she can't eat.

"No pork or beef and I'm sorry for teasing you Malcolm. I'd really enjoy coming to your home for dinner. What time?"

"Oh, five o'clock should be good. Will you be able to get a ride over?"

"Yes. My mom or dad can bring me, I'm sure. Mom's already impressed with you and I've told them all of your personal business so it's not like they don't know you."

"Ha, ha. Cool."

On Saturday — after straightenin up the house an decidin the menu — Mom an me head out for the library. We renew our cards an take out books. I get the one on soccer Nia showed me an one called *Journaling*. I know I should keep track a my thoughts on paper an that book'll show me how. I also see videos I can borrow. I get *Sarafina,* the movie Jam reminded me bout. It's kinda ole but it's a good story, involvin African kids, so I'm pretty sure Nia'll like it. I should ask her to go to the movies wit me an Dad one day.

Mom gets a big book for becomin a professional writer an where to send work. She looks over my books — OK's them — an we check out.

At the supermarket Mom and me agree it would be nice to have some fresh fish for dinner. We pick out some whitefish an white bass — get some other stuff we need — an head home.

When we get there, my mother must've decided this was a good time to teach me a few more things bout cookin cuz she tells me I'm gonna make the salad. She'd bought one a those bags wit the lettuce, carrots an radishes mixed in. She lays out all the other stuff she wants me to use on the counter.

"Put the lettuce mixture in the colander an rinse it with cold water even though the bag says *ready to eat.*"

While the stuff is drainin I use a small brush to clean a big cucumber. I rinse it an two tomatoes. I use a peeler to remove most a the skin off the cucumber an then cut it up into skinny circles. I cut the tomatoes into wedges. Then I add some baby spinach, put the salad into a big bowl, an mix up all the ingredients. "That was easy."

"You did a good job, son. Now you can make the salads twice a week. Let me add one more thing."

She sprinkles somethin called *wheat germ* on it.

"Why you wanna put *germs* on it?" I laugh, "I remember you puttin a leaf in the spaghetti but *germs?*"

"Oh, Malcolm, this kind of germ makes the salad even better

for us. You can also add tuna fish, boiled eggs, cheese and such to make a meal out of a salad. The wheat germ doesn't taste like much by itself but it's really good for you. That's also why I give you a lot of raw fruits and vegetables. They help scrub your insides."

Mom winks at me an begins puttin cornmeal an flour on the fish. Soon it's in the hot skillet an she goes around lightin candles to keep our place from smellin like it. I close our bedroom and bathroom doors for the same reason. When the fish is done, Mom lays it on paper towels to drain off the oil. She puts it in the oven to stay warm for our guest.

We get ourselves ready. I don't wanna dress up cuz I had tol Nia she didn't need to. So I keep on my jeans an put on my favorite striped tee shirt. My mom is casual too but she's put on pants wit a matchin top.

The doorbell rings an there stand Nia an her mother. I make the intros an we all sit down in the livin room. Nia's mother's name is Coral — like the animals that live in the sea an build reefs (science — all bout life).

She's shorter than Mom an honey brown like Jam. Her kinda red hair is in a fluffy afro. She's dressed casual, also. Nia looks comftable in overalls an got on a striped shirt too.

I hear her answerin one a those polite questions that older folks ask children an I realize I've missed most a the conversation. Nex I'll be designin clothes! Ms. Stellar asks:

"What is your favorite school subject, Malcolm?"

"Oh, I just about enjoy all of my classes but I especially like science because it covers everything to do with life as we know it." Ms. Stellar smiles.

"Nia pretty much feels the same way, don't you dear?"

"Yes but I think English is my favorite. Probably because I love to read and write."

Mom offers Ms. Stellar some coffee but she asks for water instead. She stands up to leave.

"I'll come back in three hours, OK? That way you two will have a nice visit. Thank you for inviting my daughter over, Carolyn. See you in a bit, sweety."

She touches Nia's head.

"It was very nice meeting you," Mom smiles.

"And yourself as well," Ms. Stellar nods. We see her out the door. Mom says:

"Nia, the food is ready. Do you feel like eating now?"

"Yes, it smells great!"

Made my stomach's day. I can't wait to get a hold a that fish!

After dinner I invite Nia to watch the videotape I borrowed but first I show her the book on journalin. "Have you ever seen *Sarafina?*"

"Why just yesterday I saw her walking down the — just kidding! I probably have because I remember thinking it was an excellent movie. I'm sure I'd enjoy seeing it again."

"Now you don't havetuh watch it. We got other stuff."

"No, *Sarafina* is fine."

"Yeah, she is pretty cute!"

"*Touché*, Master Bakersfield!"

"Yeah, uh huh!" I crow. We get comftable an watch the movie. Nia sniffles a bit over the emotional parts. I remember the first time I saw it I had strong feelins myself. I wanted to show it to Nia cuz it was bout South Africa an the African students' rebellion there. It started becuz the white government tried to make their language, *Afrikaans*, the whole country's official language. The kids was all ready to fight against the order! Sarafina's one a the bravest a the students.

The movie's a remake a what happened in 1976 wit bout 15,000 students protestin the order. Now, South Africa is free. Black African leaders are in charge. The first black president was Nelson Mandela who'd been in prison for 27 years!

When the movie is over Nia an me talk bout our favorite parts until her mother gets back. I hug Nia quickly an get her coat. Everybody says goodbye an thank you, an stuff. As they pull off, my mother gives me a *thumbs up*. "Aw, Ma, I thought you wasn't gonna tease me."

"I'm not teasing you, son. I am merely expressing my opinion of the young lady." I help wit the dishes an say: "Thanks Mom. You were on your best behavior while I entertained my guest."

"You're very welcome."

Bout one hour later, Nia calls to invite me to come visit her for lunch nex Saturday. I tell her that'll be cool cuz I won't be seein my dad until later in the day. I really wanna see what her home is like! I go into Martin's bedroom an begin typin another letter to Uncle Walter.

Dear Uncle Walter,

Hope you're doing well. Everyone is fine.

We just had my friend, Nia, over for dinner. Mom cooked some tasty fish and I made the salad! Guess it's about time for me to learn how to do stuff like that. Might not have anyone to do it for me when I'm grown and on my own—ha, ha!

I know Auntie Evelyn has been sending you pictures of Charlotte. She really is a happy baby! When I hold her she doesn't cry anymore. Auntie Ev thinks her eyes may be hazel green.

I learned something about myself. I can read the newspaper and some adult books! Nia and I met at the public library and she showed me books in the adult section that I could read and understand! I keep a dictionary next to me while I do my "adult reading" just so I won't have to get up to find a word that I don't know or comprehend. Mom and I renewed our library cards too.

The last time I saw Martin he looked good and self-satisfied. Everyone is wondering if he's going to drop out of school because he'll be sixteen soon. I got him to promise to take the GED, at least. He's too smart not to. I think he'll be all right in the long run. We all know he has a good heart.

Well, take care and know all of us are thinking about you.

Love, your nephew,
[space for my signature]

Malcolm

It gets easier everytime I write. Makes me feel better knowin he's doin OK.

I hope I never havtuh be in some stupid war.

Chapter 27

First Game

Today the basketball team's playin its first game against another team! Juan Lee, Kenyo an me is real excited! We invite our famlies an friends to come. My mother'll be there an maybe Nia will be able to stay for it. When I spoke to my dad, he said he'd try hard to make it. Kenyon's famly will try, also. It's a good thing we have some a the same friends cuz no one from Juan Lee's family would be there. Juan Lee had even asked his Uncle Mark but he already had plans.

We players is all in the locker room puttin on our team tee shirts an shorts an talkin ourselves up. The other team gotta be doin the same thing, cept *we know* we gonna win! Me, Juan Lee an Kenyon is sure to get to play, specialy Juan Lee — who turned out to be one a the best all-around players! I'm not surprised cuz he's also one a the *best break dancin b-boys* I know! He puts the *pop* in *hip hop* — ha ha! An he's real good at gettin right in your face witout touchin you. Good for basketball an Monster in the Haystack!

The game starts at 3:30 sharp! Our team is the Flash an the visitors is the Sharks. The coaches bring both teams out on the court so everyone can cheer for all of us before we play.

The startin line-up's picked an Juan Lee is gettin to play guard! The buzzer sounds an the game begins! Our center — Ryan — knocks the ball to our side an — wit Juan Lee's assist — makes it just above the key an passes the ball to Frank *"Hot Dog"* Burton — a cousin a Lakita's — *who sweetly sinks it into the net!* Our crowd screams!

I look back an see Ms. Frazier an the twins. I elbow Kenyon so he can see them too. I see Nia and Lakita in the middle row a the bleachers. I wave, then turn back to the game. The other team fails to score an the ball is back in our court. This time *we* lose the ball. The Sharks run back wit it an don't make a basket after three tries. One a our players fouls durin their last attempt. The Sharks' player gets two shots an makes both. I can tell Juan Lee really don't like that! He gets more aggressive in his blockin an helps prevent the visitors from gettin the ball back. An *flash*! We make another basket!

Soon it's halftime-wit-no-show. I look back an see my mother an father, an Auntie Evelyn wit Charlotte in her arms. I see a group a kids from school an a tall man who looks a lil familiar. On a hunch, I ask Juan Lee is it anybody else he knows here. He almost says no but then he shouts out:

"Uncle Mark!"

He's the man I noticed! He comes down to praise Juan Lee on his performance. I'm real proud for *my boy*! Mr. Frazier arrives — before he has to go to work — an switches Kenyon's glasses wit a pair that's meant for sports. Now Kenyo can really hustle!

The game continues, back an forth, back an forth. The Flash is livin up to its name. We a quicker team an have less ball turnover. Kenyon's sent in to replace a teammate who's already racked up two personal fouls. The Sharks get the ball an manage to foul him almost immediately. Kenyo makes his two an we *roar!*

When Juan Lee's taken out, I get to go in for him. I make my arms go everywhere. I try to figure out which way the player's goin even before he knows. I really can stick wit him an not foul. I assist Kenyon in makin a shot by blockin my player just as he thought he was gonna catch a loose ball. Kenyo an me slap hands as we run down the court an prepare to stop the Sharks from doin any more damage. The score's 35–32 in our favor! Juan Lee is sent back in so all three a us *is playin together!* I manage to be in the right place at the right time an sink the ball *wit nothin but net!* As the Sharks take the ball down to they side a the court, Juan Lee's first to get to the basket an *slaps the ball out a the hand a the Shark's center!* We miss when one a our players tries to score above the key. But we get the ball back on rebound an wit only one minute lef, I charge down the court an pass the ball to *"Karlos wit a K"* an swoosh, we got another two points! We win the game by seven points! 39–32!

After shakin hands wit the other team, we leave the court on our way to the locker room. I see my mom an dad cheerin; Lakita an Nia too. We hurry up an get out to *our fans* as soon as the coaches finish congratulatin us.

My mom an dad hug me. Auntie Evelyn holds Charlotte out for a kiss. Nia hugs me too an says she's leavin cuz her mom tol her to be ready to go by five.

We all meet Juan Lee's Uncle Mark an his lady friend, Janean. Mr. Mark Lee has heard so much bout us that he already knows who's who. I shake his hand an tell him to be sure to make it to as many games as possible. He smiles at me an maybe he understands what I'm really tryin to say. He favors Juan Lee but he's on the tall side an Juan Lee is on the almost short side. They leave together to celebrate at a restaurant somewhere. Ms. Frazier takes Kenyon an the twins home where a special meal is waitin. Mom an me decide to get some Chinese food take-out an go home.

"Good game, son!" Dad tells me as he's leavin. Then Martin appears. He arrived late but claims he did get to see me play. "Come wit us to the house." I say.

"OK. For a minute."

I'm happy he showed up cuz we ain spoke since I tol him I knew he was runnin numbers. I think bout Mom's poem for Martin when he was a baby. It goes:

"My Baby

Look how he smiles!
He can light up the room,
And banish all feelings of worry and gloom.
A sweet, happy baby,
This mother's been blessed.
She'll raise him up right
To meet any test."

Knowin Martin, he's got a copy of it but I bet he never tol it to nobody.

Chapter 28

Brothas

Martin stays after when we finish eatin. I'm glad he does cuz I want some time wit him an me alone. "Hey bro, I apologize for tellin you what to do wit your life. But I wantchu to *promise* me again that if you drop out a school you'll get a GED."

"I'll *do* it, *OK?*"

"Cool."

I can almost picture Martin the way he looked when he was my age. Tonight, for some reason, he seems a lil off-key. We in his ole room an I'm walkin around touchin stuff he lef behind. Mom might let someone visitin sleep in his bed but the room stays almost as if he still lives wit us.

Martin seems real tired out. He's layin sideways cross the bed, his head on a pillow propped up against the wall. I sit down nex to him an neither a us say anything for a long while. We just brothas together.

Mom is busy in the kitchen puttin food away. I get the feelin she's tryin to give us some alone time. Martin's so quiet I havtuh look at him close to make sure he's still awake. He opens his eyes an says:

"How can I help you?"

"A *hug* would do. I won't tell nobody." Martin laughs an

we hug just like we used to do when we was younger.

"You want me to ask Mom if you can spend the night?"

"Nah, I might ask her myself," he yawns.

As if on cue, Mom appears in the doorway.

"Would you like to spend the night, oh-firstborn-son of mine?"

"Yeah, Mom, if it's OK witchu."

"Yeah, it's OK *wit* me." Mom chuckles. "I can stand to see you two together for a while. *And it's actually just the three of us!* This hasn't happened since *forever!*"

I go find Martin a double-x tee shirt to sleep in an throw it on his head.

"Would you two like to watch a movie?"

"Whatchu got?"

Martin wonders, tryin to sound excited.

"*Finding Forrester.* It has something for *everyone!* Basketball, school, a very talented young man, a grouchy old man, and a happy mother!"

I grin an ask, "Can we have popcorn?"

"Sure can!" Mom says like she's in a ole TV commercial. She goes to nuke some in the microwave.

"Can you hang, man?" I whisper to Martin. He's still lookin tired.

"Yeah, sure. Get ready — though — cuz you know the movie's gonna have some serious lesson for us to learn. Las time it was Akeelah and the Bee."

"Yeah, I know. But it makes her happy."

"I should ask if she got anything on break dancin."

"Mom probly *do* know how to do ole school step from back in the day."

We laugh an go into the livin room. Mom brings in one big bowl a popcorn wit smaller bowls for each a us. I put the DVD into the player an sit back.

The movie was real good! I'm hopin Martin liked it too an ain just fakin. It makes me think bout how my life could be. Shoot, I got the grades, the talent an can even play a lil basketball. I can make it in some special school for smarter kids. Martin could too if he wanted. We talk some bout the movie so Mom'd know we didn't miss the message, then we fellas go to bed.

The nex mornin, Mom, Martin an me have breakfast together. Martin's still in no hurry to leave. It's a nice visit for us. When he's ready to go, I leave out wit him an tell him bout Jam an me goin to the concert.

"Oh, yeah? How'd that go?"

"Martin, *Jam is cool*, man! Nex time he asks you to go somewhere, just do it! I always learn somethin from him bout big an lil things. I think him an Mom gonna wind up married."

"Then you'll havtuh answer to *two* fathers."

"I'll still be the same person. I don't do much cept go to school an overachieve. What they gonna complain bout?"

"Don't worry, they'll find somethin."

"Anyway, man, you welcome to join me wit whoever I'm wit, Jam *or* Dad. Then you can be fifteen for a few hours."

"That might get to be habit formin."

"Mart-*in!*"

"Aw, shut up *bonehead!* You soun like Rich or somebody," Martin laughs.

At lease I got him to smile. "But, seriously, bro-man, I'll get in touch witchu when we get ready to do somethin. I'll try to give you a coupla day's notice, ah'ight?"

"Yeah, right, OK. Look, I'm goin over to Jess' house so unless you wanna see him, we can part ways now."

"Ah'ight. Just think bout my offer." We sock each other in the shoulder an I sprint back toward the house. On the way, I notice a car out the corner a my eye drivin slowly nex to me. I'm gettin scared til I look an see it's *Jam* grinnin at me in a *new van!* I lean into the window an say, "I must've just spoke you up! Me an Martin was talkin an I was tryin to get him to hang out wit us the nex time we doin somethin!"

"You don't say? What'd he think?"

"He's thinkin bout it. Just have to let it marinate some."

"You know, you *can* get in my ride. I'm goin your way to see this *beautiful, intelligent, wonderful creature* that for some strange reason happens to love me. *Me!* Only thing is she's got this know-it-all son that lives with her. I havtuh get rid a that kid somehow! You got any ideas?"

I laugh the rest a the way home.

Chapter 29

Lunch

Today's the day I visit Nia at her house. My mother drives me there but she's got some errands to do for Granma Sil, so she arranged for Jam to pick me up since he was free an comin that way.

We arrive at the house an Ms. Stellar meets us at the door. My mother thanks her for the invitation an explains why she can't stay. She leaves an Ms. Stellar says:

"Nia should be down in a minute, Malcolm. Let me take your coat."

As soon as she hears Nia comin down the stairs, Ms. Stellar excuses herself an disappears into the kitchen. I go over to the piano in the livin room an havtuh stop myself from touchin it. It's the same wit all the African lookin statues and pictures. Nia comes over to me an says:

"Hey homey! Great to see you! Been so long, yet it seems like only yesterday!"

"It was yesterday, you *knucklehead!*"

"Oh, I see we have some affection for the Three Stooges, nyuk, nyuk, nyuk."

I'm laughin now, "OK, I admit to bein a fan. I got a VHS tape, all Stooges."

"Who's your favorite?"

"Moe, cuz he's so impatient an angry."

"Mine's Curly. I like it when he hums or sings, or whatever you call what he does. C'mon, lets go into … *The Media Room.*"

"Nia, you jokin, right? Ya'll don't really call it that!"

"*Psych!* No, we don't. I'm just doing my usual — *ha, ha, ha!*"

"Yeah, that's right, lie to your guest." The room seems to actualy deserve the name, though. There's one wall full a books, tapes an DVD's. There's also a large, flat screen TV wit a combo DVD an VHS player, a computer, an a printer. Reminds me some a my cousins' crib. Nia grins an says:

"Actually, this is my parents' idea of a den. There's a similar room upstairs but with more books. That's where I do my homework and stuff."

"Do you have a TV in your bedroom too?"

"Nope. That's against the rules around here. My parents don't believe children should have a TV *or* a computer in their bedrooms. But I do have a *noice* music system."

"Do you know how to play the piano?"

"Not very well. I don't even touch it lately. I'm not talented in that way. But my dad plays. He also writes poems. I can recite one for you later."

"OK. Jam said he might be able to teach me how to play the congas. You know, those big drums you play wit your hands?"

"Yeah. I can picture you doing that. "

"So why can't you have a TV in your bedroom? That seems weird to me. I mean, I don't have one in mine either but it's cuz my mom only buys things that are really necessary."

"My parents don't want me watching TV when I'm supposed to be sleeping. Also — if I'm being punished — it makes the message louder and clearer. I'm not even supposed to be listening to any music. Of course, *they* have a TV in *their* bedroom.

My dad complains that regular TV has become almost as bad as some of the stuff on cable and I have to agree with him. The shows that come on starting from eight p.m. are *way too racy* and you can see commercials any time of the day that are too."

"What does *racy* mean?" I'm tryin to imagine what Nia coulda done to get punished.

"Sexual stuff. My father says it's cause regular TV is trying to compete with cable and all. My parents trust me when they're busy. But I have sneaked a bit onto some of the other channels and it's twenty-four hours of whatever you can think of and even what you can't! Just the dance videos are almost *pornographic!* I mean, I'm interested cause I'm curious but I don't want to get my education that way. But guess what, *we're still children!* We don't need to have that stuff up in our faces *all* of the time! And I'd rather learn about sex from my parents, or a class ... or even a biological book."

"Scientific, right? That way you can understand how things work an don't get all mixed up. How many kids know enough bout how to protect theyselves from disease? Some *adults* don't even do what they sposed to do to stay healthy. I mean — *you could die!* My mother says it's best to be grown so you can be — responsible — even if you a man. I heard her talkin to Martin bout how would he feel if some girl — he didn't at lease care bout — had his baby. She don't regret havin him but she wishes she'd waited like my Granma Silver taught her. She didn't know Martin's father was gonna be a *sometimes dad*. She had-tuh pass up goin to college cuz she had Martin to take care a."

"That must've been pretty tough for her to go through."

"Yep. But I know I can talk to her bout anything. She seems a lil nervous bout me growin up, though. I wanna tell her I pretty much know bout sex but that I'll respect her advice, anyway."

"There's *always* pressure for kids to experiment with *something.* I guess some grown-ups forget that."

"What does pornographic mean? Naked pictures?"

"Yeah but a lot of freakish junk. My parents had a talk with me about it because sometimes children are involved. They want me to be aware and safe."

"Daaang! I read an hear bout junk like that in the paper an on the news. You know what else is weird? The way the TV shows have kids actin an dressin like they grown. If I had a sista, she wouldn't even fix her mouth to ask for some a the stuff them young girls be wearin. An my pants can be baggy but *I better not ever be saggin*!"

"I guess I'm out of it cause I can't understand why boys — and men — want to show their *underwear* or *naked butt* in public! Maybe it's for the same reason you see bra straps and thongs showing on girls and women." Nia shrugs.

"Most a the kids on TV treat the adults like they dirt or real stupid. An some shows that are sposed to be for grown folks'll have a kid in it talkin an hearin stuff. It's seems like anything's OK if the kids aren't *doin* the things. I watch some a the sit-coms cuz they funny, an even old re-runs that were made for adults. I know they just stupid shows and I don't take any a them seriously. But you can best believe the networks don't care that they come on *just in time for your child to view after school!*"

"Ha, ha! Did you know that cartoons were originally meant for adults?"

"Naw. I never heard that one."

"It's true. But it's hard to tell which ones are, or should be. And, we can't forget the Internet. I've found some sites that were *really scary* masquerading as something for kids! I always leave them *ASAP!* I don't even visit chat rooms cause I don't want to be corresponding with some adult in disguise or get a virus! But even so, my family understands that having the freedom to find all information is a good thing."

"Uh huh. Have you ever watched a soap opera?"

"Oh, those are for adults too. But some kids run home so they don't *miss their stories*." Nia whined an imitation.

"Those shows are silly to me. How much can happen to one person in *one day?* I watched some a them when I was home sick an somebody was always messin wit somebody else's man or woman. I read in one a my mom's magazines that a lot a men even watch soaps."

"*You're kidding!*"

"Nope. They even got soaps that's actualy *made* for teenagers. I pretty much feel that if somethin has a continuin story, it *could* be a soap. I hate some a those 'reality shows' too. Folks airin out all they bizness or actin stupid just to get on TV."

"I confess; I do like some of them. What about music? I don't dance to anything that puts females down."

"Yeah, I understand. I havtuh catch myself cuz I might start rappin some a that junk. All rap ain like that, though. The stuff that gets the airplay usely be rough but it's some that's more positive comin out now like ole hip hop was — accordin to Martin"

"So, bud, what do you wanna do til it's time to eat?"

"We could play one a those games you got in the corner."

"Which one? I'm really good at checkers. Or would you rather play Scrabble?"

"What bout chess?"

"Still learning that one."

"I don't know how to play it anyway!"

"We're both good at spelling so let's try Scrabble."

"OK. Get out the dictionary for challenges."

"We got one that's made for the game."

"*'Noice, wanna'* an *'we got one'*? Guess I'm rubbin off on you!"

"You switch up too. I jus don't say anything, Mr. Bilingual."

"You are exactly right, my dear. So let's not squabble. *Let's play Scrabble!*"

"Quite right, Mr. B. It's such a *delight* to have fun with words!"

We play for bout thirty minutes. Both a us get some good words made an Nia's leadin by five points. We stop when it's time to eat.

Ms. Stellar serves us "*rice pilaf* (mushrooms, onions an stuff in it)," some small chickens she had cut in half, an a spinach salad. The salad dressin is some I'd never tasted before. "Ms. Stellar, what kind of dressing is this?"

"Raspberry *vinaigrette*, Malcolm. You like it?"

"Yes, I like sour and sweet tastes together. Where did you get such small chickens, Ms. Stellar?"

"They're called *Cornish* hens. You can buy them in grocery stores."

"Have some lemonade." Nia offers.

"Ooh, *more* sour and sweet!" Everything's real good an I compliment Ms. Stellar on the meal.

"Oh, thanks dear but I didn't make the meal — Nia did."

 Nia stands up an takes a bow.

"Mom helped me with the hens, however."

"I'm *most impressed!*"

"So, should we finish playing Scrabble?"

"How about we play straight checkers so I can see how good you are?"

"All right. But by the *real* rules."

We go back to the den. I state: "No 'blowin'. You havtuh take all your jumps, an black goes first. An we switch colors after each game."

"Right, and only going backward when you have another jump to make after the first forward one — and — only kings can go everywhere but just one square at a time."

I win the first three games an Nia wins the nex two. We keep playin until we play twenty games. I'm declared the winner by eight. "I play checkers wit my dad an some a the customers at the barbershop he takes me to. An I also play wit the Checkers to Chess Club that Mr. Masomakali's Special Ed class sponsors. Believe me, 'learning disabled' does not mean dumb! So, you didn't do *too* bad."

"Do any girls from the learning differently classes play?"

"The … oh, I get it. Not too many a them. They think it's more of a male thing."

"Speaking of which, my dad and two uncles went to the hardware store so you probly won't get to meet them this time."

"Your father's brothas?"

"Yep. They're triplets but they aren't identical so they don't really look the same. They have rhyming names, though."

"What are they?"

" My dad's Chance and my uncles are Vance and Lance. You ready for me to tell you the poem?"

"Sure."

"It's called, "This Gift." My dad wrote it inside a book he gave me."

"What kinda book?"

"A *thesaurus*."

"Thorry. A what?"

"Malcolm, I know you already know what one is."

"Still gettin back atchu for all your teasin. Tell me the poem."

"OK …

'This Gift

This gift does not appear to be much,
When compared to dresses, dolls and such.
But within these pages, you shall surely find,
The ingredients to help develop your mind.
And as you grow older, you will resort to it more,
For the pursuit of knowledge is an ever-widening door.
Skeptics may scorn the above remark,
Let those non-believers remain perpetually in the dark.
Ignorance is theirs to be forever nourished in their breast,
For they will never know or envision life at its best.
Time alone will prove the accuracy of these statements,
my dear.
The all-powerful human mind is indeed The Last Frontier.'"

"Wow! My mom would *love* that! An you memorized it too!"

"I'll give you a copy for her."

"Cool! Hey, I've been meanin to ask — why don't you go to the junior high near here?"

"My mom and dad wanted me to go to your school cause they felt it would be easier for me to fit in there. Y'know, children can be so cruel and all that."

The doorbell rings an it's Jam come to get me. I re-introduce him to Ms. Stellar. Nia gets my coat. I thank Ms. Stellar for havin me over an give Nia a hug.

She sings:

"See you next week!"

We had enjoyed ourselves doin nothin special. Just playin low tech games. No electronics, no complicated parts. I know it's our combination.

Most anything can be fun when you wit somebody you like.

"I gotta stop by the music store before I take you home, *young brotha.*"

"Ah'ight."

The place's actualy called The Music Store. It looks like they got any an everything a musician could ever want! I walk around gently touchin instruments an stuff, tryin to take it all in. Jam's only buyin a few sets a drumsticks so he's ready to go before I get to finish lookin. When he starts up his van an the music comes on, I ask him what group's playin. He proudly booms:

"My band, *Jazzatude!* You like?"

"Yeah, I like! I thought y'all only played jazz." I try to sound knowledgeable.

"This *is* jazz. It's a kind called *straight-ahead.* You could call it *classical jazz.*"

So even jazz has diffrent categories. I pat my fingers on the dashboard to the rhythm an listen harder for the drums.

When we reach the house I grin: "My compliments to the drummer."

Jam laughs as we slap hands. I watch him go. Then I get ready for my visit wit my dad.

Chapter 30

Uncovered

I guess it couldn't remain a secret for much longer. One a the kids in the class been watchin me an Nia real close. She sees how I let Nia hold my new pencils before usin them. She also knows her own work is better cuz she's gettin more C+'s than she ever had. She's spoiled lazy an ignorant actin in school. Her name's Jade Green. She's always liked me for more'n a friend but I barely speak to her cuz she's mean an phony. Plus — she's one a those kids that likes to pick on the ones doin good.

I hear Jade say she's been testin her pencils from home. She's noticed that even her handwritin improves when she uses the ones Nia touched. She starts tellin everybody that Nia's a witch.

"How else can you explain her bein able to do so many things so good?" Jade tells anybody listenin. "An you ever known Malcolm Bakersfield to hang out wit a girl? She must got him under some kinda *spell!*"

All this talk makes more an more kids suspicious. Turns out some been jealous a Nia all along. It makes me angry! Nia just shrugs an says she's used to it an I shouldn't let it bother me. But I *am* bothered. Part a why it's even happenin is my fault! Why can't the class just be happy that everybody's grades is better an leave it at that? An — as if it wasn't bad enough — we got kids from other classes tryin to figure out what makes our class so special. The Collector's found a way to profit from that. He'd started up his trash pickin again. He digs in the basket right after Nia throws out pencils an gets kids from the other classes to give him candy — or even money — for them. An a course — they grades improve an Nia gets less privacy. Even some teachers have her hold they ink pens — which doesn't work — I figure. To my mind, only the pencils can be magic. An they probly only work for kids.

One day the principal — herself — walks in askin to see Nia. Nia leaves witout lookin back. It's quiet as death in the room.

Jade whispers to nobody in particular:

"Not 'Ms. Perfect!'"

The whole room starts buzzin. Ms. Winston gets the class to settle down wit the threat of a writin punishment usin one a her new pencils (untouched by Nia) which means it would take at lease a hour to do. She also tells *Miss Jade* to stop instigatin. I look back at Juan Lee to see how he's takin all this. He looks straight at me an nods his head a few times. I know me an him still cool.

I'm worryin bout Nia. What does the principal want her for? I ask to go to the lavatory cuz it's on the way to the office. I *havtuh* check on Nia. I pass by once then turn back an see her sittin on the bench. I whisper, "Are you in trouble?"

She whispers back:

"No, Ms. Drench just wants me to touch her pencils. It's no big deal."

Still, she sounds a lil down to me. I go back to class an feel bad for my friend. Bein used by the principal. What nex, a TV appearance? Nia can't help it. She's a giver in a world a takers.

When she returns to class, the buzzin starts up again. Ms. Winston tells Nia to come to her desk.

"Are you all right, dear?"

"Yes, ma'am," she answers quietly.

At lunch time, I ask Nia to tell me if anything else happened while she was wit the principal. She says Ms. Drench was real happy to have her there. She tol her that from what she understood Nia had the power to make every student do better work. Nia tried to explain that it wasn't her doin. But *"Ole Drench"* just kept on praisin her.

Nia did a good impression a Ms. Drench while tellin me more bout what happened. She mocked:

"'You are putting our school on the map! We have improved *one hundred percent* because of *your ability* and you, my dear, are just too *modest* to admit it. I don't know how you manage to do the things you do but I *would like* to know. From you. *Right now.*'"

Nia rolls her eyes, her voice returnin to normal.

"I told Ms. Drench again I was not making pencils magical."

She puts her Drench voice back on:

"'Well, if you want to keep *denying* this, I can't *force* you to admit to anything. Just be prepared for being *recognized by the whole school* soon. Now, *please* follow me.'"

Nia shrugs in wonder. She continues:

"Then we go to the storage room where I touch every pencil with a black lead *while they're still in the box!* Ms. Drench smiles at me like I really did something, thanks me and sends me back to class. You know what?"

"What?"

"People like Ms. Drench are *very dangerous.*"

"Why's that?"

"Because they can look and act pleasantly — but they aren't that way for real. All while I was with her, she kept on trying to make me feel *privileged* when she was just using me. Reminds me of when I was sent to the office at my last school for drawing in class. My work was done and I had read every book on the class library shelf (We weren't allowed to leave class to use the school's library.) So — other than reading the dictionary, which the teacher said was a waste of time — I started to draw. I guess I should've asked for more work or brought a new book to read. Anyway, the teacher announced it was not time for art and sent me to the office. Guess what the principal had me do while I was there?"

"What?"

"Draw pictures on folded papers that she would use as greeting cards."

"That's messed up!"

"That's how Ms. Drench seems to think. She must not really feel I'm that smart if she believes I don't know when I'm being used."

Chapter 31

Misunderstood

The followin day, Nia don't have much to say. She's bein stared at or ignored by most a the class. I don't get a chance to talk wit her until lunchtime. We sit on a bench an don't speak for the first few minutes.

Then, Nia announces:

"I'm going to have to change schools again. Just because things seem to happen by me doing one thing or another, I am thought to be the only one responsible. Oh, it is always something good and it would be easier if I would just agree and say what people want to hear *but I am not a liar.*

At my last school — all the adults who could — began spending time tutoring students before and after school and volunteering to help in other ways. It happened when I told every class in the school to beg mother, father, and whomever, to help if they could. This was something the principal had been trying to achieve since he arrived years before. When it actually began to happen, he found out from some of the students that I told them to ask their families and neighbors to help. They told him I said to beg as if they were asking for a special toy or some candy. And that is what they did and that is how it happened."

"Well, Nia you did get things started."

"Yes but if the children had not done what I suggested, none of it would have happened so quickly. Don't you see that? I just came up with the idea and influenced the children to want to do better and make their families realize they were needed to get more involved "

"So what was wrong about that?"

"The fact that everyone held me responsible for what 500 children did! I just put an idea in their heads! Suddenly, I became some type of celebrity, which had a negative side too. That's not what I had in mind, to be treated as a hero! *The volunteers were the heroes! The victors were the children!* It seems as if nothing will ever change!"

"But Nia, you've had a big influence here. Look at how well everyone's doing! We all *know* your pencils are magic. And, according to the grades and test scores, you can't deny that you caused it to happen!"

"Yes, I can because *the pencils are not magical.*"

"*Aw, man!* Nia, even I know they are but every time I ask you about it, you pretend not to know what I'm saying. What about the fight you almost had with Lakita? I know you commanded her to stop wanting to. What about the time you and I were talking and no one else was moving? You've got *something* going on and *I know it.*"

"Well, Malcolm, *if you — of all people —* won't believe me when I say the pencils are not magical, *no one* will. And those other things you mentioned, you may have imagined them, right?"

"*I don't think so.* But look, I'm your bud no matter what, OK? I don't care if you've got special powers or not. It's all been to the good, so I ain got no beef witchu, ah' ight?"

"All right. Thank you Malcolm. You *are* one of the *best friends* I've ever had."

"An I plan to keep it that way. This thing'll blow over.

Knowin Ole Drench, she'll be takin credit for it all soon, anyway. But Juan Lee, Kenyon, and me got your back."

"Thanks. It's about time to go back in." She sighs.

I touch Nia's hand an tell her to cheer up. But I feel sorry bout the lie I just tol. Things is gonna get much worse before they get better.

Right before dismissal, we all get flyers to take home bout a special assembly for parents an guardians. It's for this comin Friday afternoon. I wonder if it got anything to do wit Nia.

Most likely it does.

Chapter 32

Fish Bowl

Nia arrives late to school. She drops me a note sayin she did it on purpose. While she walks to her seat, someone makes a comment. I don't know what was said but a lotta kids are laughin. Probly big mouth Jade again. The thing that amazes me is how hateful so many a our classmates is actin. Nia ain done nothin bad to nobody. But you'd think she was a demon the way most kids is treatin her.

I tol my mother yesterday when I first noticed the meanness. She believes it's all from jealousy.

"Sometimes being a good person and helping others backfires. Nia is a giving person and while everyone's happy to do better, they resent her being the one seeming to help them. Most people — believe it or not — don't like depending on or being beholden to someone else. So, they find fault with — and blame — the helper to make themselves feel better. Now even though I think your imagination is involved here, it appears that some people truly believe Nia has special powers. And, I figure it's making most of them very uncomfortable."

At lunchtime, I repeat to Nia what my mother said — cept for the part bout Nia havin special powers. She nods her head an says it makes sense.

"It's sad, because if it wasn't for that way of thinking people might be more helpful and happier. But I guess some can't bring themselves to believe there are others who just like to help and feel good from just doing that. Maybe if we asked for pay we'd be more appreciated."

I'm glad she included me. "You think of me that way, right?"

"Of course I do! You've been nothing but a good, helpful friend to me and others, Malcolm."

Lakita swoops over an says: "Don't let the turkeys getchu down! *Fly like a eagle!"*

She grabs a loose basketball an makes a lay-up shot an continues to play. Lakita's more amped up than usual because Coach Pruitt tol her she could practice wit the team on the days we don't have a game. Nia wasn't surprised when I told her that.

In class, Nia asks permission to leave the room. She wants to get away from all the anger aimed at her, I figure.

When it's time to go home, Kenyon, Juan Lee, an me walk her to the bus stop. It's a good thing we did cuz a group a kids is followin behind us an they don't seem friendly. They hang around like they expect us to leave Nia. But we stand our ground right around her. After a bit a teasin an semi-threats the group shuffles away. Nia's bus shows up an she waves *bye* as she gets on. When the bus pulls off, me an my boys pump our right fists in the air for her.

Chapter 33

Friendship

At night, I call Nia as late as I dare to make sure she's comin to school tomorrow. She don't sound any more cheerful than she did the earlier part a the day. So I'm still kinda worried when I hang up even though she said she'd be there.

My mother comes in late from work an immediately asks me what's wrong.

"Nia's goin to another school."

"Why?"

"The *same* stuff! Now the whole school believes she has some magical effect on pencils that make everyone do better."

"An what do you think about that?"

"Mom, I don't know! I don't know *what* to believe. A lot of good things have happened since Nia's been at Gillespie. I don't believe she's actually lied to me but it's possible cause some things I really can't explain happened right before my eyes!"

"Does Nia still consider you to be on her side?"

"Yes. She's too great of a person for me not to help."

"Well, that's good. She's going to need whatever friends she has now until her parents decide what to do."

"Yeah, I know."

My mother hugs me.

"Goodnight, sweetheart."

"Night, Ma."

When I finally get to sleep, I dream bout Nia an the whole situation:

Every kid in the school wants a piece a Nia. Just pencils ain enough, no more. Nia tries to escape from them but they follow her everywhere. She runs out a the school an into a long tunnel. Kids still follow beggin her for all kinds a reasons. One wants her to teach him how to draw, another wants to learn how to sing, an they all want instant service an talent! When she refuses them they continue to chase her an call her stingy.

"You owe us!" they all scream.

"Leave me alone! Go help yourselves!" Nia hollers.

She leaves them behind so fast it's as if she's flyin! I'm followin the sound a her voice tryin to see if I can find her an help somehow. The kids' screamin, demandin, an beggin never stops.

"You got so many gifts, you havtuh share them wit us."

"It ain fair that one person should have so much."

"Help us! Help us!"

"We know you can."

"We've seen it!"

"Help me!"

"No, help me first!"

"We need you!"

"Help!"

"Help!"

Just as I get to Nia, the fastest kids catch up an try to grab her. Nia starts risin up, her feet leavin the ground. She looks surprised when she ends up hoverin under the ceilin! I'm yellin an runnin back an forth tryin to get her attention. I hear her tellin the kids to stay back. I see the girls who used to play wit her hair snappin scissors. Nia howls in rage. She begins to protect herself. She knocks children down wit just a wave a her hand.

"Nia, please stop!" I beg her.

"This is not your business! You don't know what it's like to be me!"

"I know you the best a anybody at school!" I argue back.

"You don't believe me either! Don't make me hurt you, Malcolm! Leave me alone!"

She flies back an forth under the ceilin like a bird in a cage. I notice there's no longer a way out. I'm scared for her an for me.

"Nia don't wanna hurt nobody else but you ain givin her no other choice!" I holler at the kids while they try to catch her. Suddenly, they all rush me! They run over me; stand on me. I can't breathe. . .

I wake up from the nightmare breathin hard an my heart's beatin real fast. It takes me a long time to get back to sleep.

Chapter 34

Escape

The nex day I wait out in the hall for Nia. When I see her hurryin to class, I feel relief. I'm still worried bout what's to come but I wanna see her in school more.

"Hey buddy, gladtuh see you!"

"Yeah, glad to see you too."

"Still think you havtuh leave, huh?"

"Yes. You seem to forget that everyone knows I've been used by Ms. Drench and are plotting what else they can get from me."

"Well, what bout me, Kenyon an Juan Lee? I keep tellin you we care bout you an don't want you to go. My brotha Martin even knows bout you an he can keep some a the heat off."

"Look, Malcolm, you just don't understand. The fact that most everyone here thinks I perform magic means they won't rest until I reveal all of my gifts. I can't make someone become an artist or writer immediately. I can't even have a normal relationship anymore with anyone here but you. My time at Gillespie is over. I lose my *purpose* once folk decide I can *give* them what they want. My intent is to *encourage others to bring forth their best selves.* I'm willing to help but the effort is up to the person."

I had never heard Nia talk bout havin a purpose before.

Also, how did she come so close to talkin bout the dream I had last night? "So you're just gonna up an go?"

"Yes."

"Well, I'll really miss you."

"No you won't."

"Huh? *How do you know?*"

"Because I'll always be with you in spirit.

"You mean we can keep in touch an stuff?"

"Yes, Malcolm. I will keep in touch no matter what and I promise you'll see me again no matter where I go. Just keep me close as you do the poem your mother wrote about you."

"Well, that makes me feel better but I really wish you would stay." Then I try to remember if I'd ever shared the poem wit her. How else could she know bout it?

"All you have to do is remember we'll be in touch and that I'll *never* forget you."

Nia reaches in her purse an pulls out one a those plastic yellow stars that glow in the dark. She looks up at me an says:

"Here's something to help you remember."

I slowly take the star off her palm and put it in my pocket. Then she treats me to one a those beautiful smiles.

Ms. Winston comes to the door an asks:

"When are you two going to come into the classroom?"

"Now." we both answer together. As we enter the room, Jade an the other gossips start up until Ms. Winston tells them firmly to be quiet. I'm kinda surprised that no adults have showed up since Nia's become common knowledge. They'll probly come right before it's time to for us to leave. I hope Nia's mother picks her up early.

Durin math class a messenger delivers a note to Mr. Burns.

He looks at it an calls Nia up to the desk an gives it to her witout another word. She takes her books an goes out a the classroom. When she comes back, she has her coat an back-pack. The backpack looks slack, so I figure she's left her books in her locker. A lil while after, she gets up an drops a note on my desk.

The note says: *"My mother is picking me up in about ten minutes."* Since any lil thing she does is news, a lot a the kids is watchin to see if they can figure out what's goin on. When another five minutes pass, Nia gets up an goes out the door. Jade an her crew start talkin bout Nia havin special priv-leges an stuff. Mr. Burns clears his throat meaningfully an the noise stops.

When it's time for us to return to homeroom, I see a lot a adults kinda circlin around inside the school. I'm thank-ful Nia's safe.

That evening she tells me on the phone that walkin through the hallway was like bein on death row or somethin. The kids in the hall stared at her as if she had a sack full a pres-ents to pass out. The kindergardeners she worked wit smiled an whispered to her as they snaked through the hallway wit arms folded. Nia said she felt each a their upturned faces reflectin her love for them; she was still they Future Teacher. She complimented them on they one-behind-the-other line. She tol their teacher she wouldn't be able to come help. Mr. Shine nodded and said he understood. Nia continued down the seemingly endless hallway to the front door where her mother was waitin for her. She slid fast inside the car, almost bumpin her head.

"Are you comin to school tomorrow?"

"I guess so. Probably."

I tell her to have a good night's sleep an hang up. Then, I think bout how well will I sleep tonight? There's a basketball game tomorrow an we gonna play another team in our gym again. I plan to work myself real hard. Might help me deal better wit everythin goin on an get to sleep earlier. For tonight, I'll take a hot bath an drink some a Mom's *chamomile* relaxation tea (wit her permission, a course).

Chapter 35

Missin

I'd slept OK so I'm able to catch up wit Juan Lee an get to school on time.

I wait for Nia to come so I can talk to her again before goin into the room. I give up after the bell rings. When she don't show up by nine, I figure she ain comin. Probly for the best.

Even Nia's absence is cause for talk. I try hard to ignore the comments cuz I don't wanna do anything stupid like glue Jade's mouth shut. I pull out a for-my-eyes-only list I made a the words that fit 'Jaw Jackin Jade': *lip smacking, wise cracking, front backing, fact hacking, brain lacking.* I add a few to it to work on later: *pack, quack, racket, sack, wack, whack, yacking.* Now that I've got that out a my system it's easier to remain calm.

I concentrate on my schoolwork an try to get as deep as possible into it. I can still hear some a the remarks, though. An since Nia ain available to pick on, I become the target.

"Oh, look at poor Jack witout Jill."

"What's he gonna do?"

"Boo, hoo, hoo!"

I ignore them an continue wit my work. When I finish, I find my new notepad an start on my self-improvement plan.

I get a dictionary from the bookshelf an return to my seat. I open it to any page an make sentences after readin the definition a words I don't know. I deliberately don't read the example sentences until I've written mine. When I get tired a that, I play the game where you make up words from one long word. It's called *ana* somethin. You can only use the letters in the chosen word an if it only has one e that's all the e's you can use in your new word. You can't use proper names, either. It's more fun to do wit a group but I'm enjoyin entertainin myself. When I remember the name — anagrams — I look it up to be sure. Then I notice my concentration has become so deep, I barely hear the whispers an other noises from the class.

At lunch, I play basketball the whole time we outside. Kenyo an Juan Lee know I'm tryin to maintain, so they keep the conversatin light. As we gettin ready to go into the buildin, Lakita rushes over to ask me bout 'her girl, Nia'. I tell her she's OK (like I know). I'm gonna call her as soon as I get home. *Oops!* Good thing I remembered to bring my gym shoes an uniform! I had almost forgotten bout today's game cuz we playin on Thursday instead a Friday.

The game ain as excitin an fast paced as our last one. It was sposed to be our first away game but we can't play at the other school cuz its gym is bein painted.

This team ain nothin like they name; the Blazers. They ain fast or aggressive. Our coaches feel they a lil intimidated cuz they come from a part a the city that's near the suburbs. But that ain our concern. Juan Lee, Kenyon an me get to play at the same time again for a bit. Altogether on the floor, we three score ten points. Kenyo makes a shot from half court! Juan Lee steals the ball four times an makes it twice to the hoop an through. I make one hook shot an slap the ball from the other team's scorin attempts twice. By game's end, the score is 58-40. Some a our second stringers — who usualy ride the bench — even get a chance to play. We all good winners, though. We shake every hand a the other team an don't boast. Save all that for the locker room!

My mom had come late. Mr. Frazier an Juan Lee's Uncle Mark is there. We all goin to celebrate over to the Frazier's house but first, me an Mom pick up some sides from the Hot Plate Restaurant. We wanna make sure there's enough food for everybody.

After our dinner, I ask Ms. Frazier can I use her phone.

She says, "Course you can, baby!" I smile an bend my head down. I call Nia cuz I hadtuh know how she was doin.

"Hi, Ms. Stellar. This is Malcolm. May I speak to Nia?"

"Sure, Malcolm. Just a moment … Here she is."

"Hi, Nia. Guess your mom was on the phone."

"She was about to get off anyway or she would've asked you to call back."

"So how are you? Even Lakita was wonderin."

"I'm OK, just didn't feel up to the staring, glaring and gossiping."

"I thought you just wanted an excuse to watch soap operas — ha, ha. So are you comin tomorrow?"

"Yeah, I'll be there. It'll be my last day."

"Um, we won the game, 58-40. The other team just couldn't hang."

"That's great! Sorry I missed it."

"Well, I'ma letchu go. I'm at Kenyon's house. We havin a lil celebration dinner."

"OK. Martin didn't make it?"

"Nah, it's ah'ight though. He must've had somethin else to do."

"Thanks for calling. Sleep well."

"You too buddy. See you tomorrow." I slowly hang up the phone. Now I'm thinkin how'd she know I'm havin trouble sleepin? She must be sharin room in my head wit my mom.

I go back into the dinin room. I didn't wanna tell Nia bout the parents hangin around the school earlier. I'm still wonderin an dreadin what's gonna happen tomorrow.

An I plan to help Nia in any way possible.

Chapter 36

The Purpose

The nex day a bunch a adults show up to the school for the assembly. Assistant Principal Thayer is guidin them straight into the auditorium. I stay at my locker cuz it's close by. I hear a woman mumblin bout some strange child in her daughter's class. She sounds mean. Probly *"Jaw-jackin's"* mother.

I got the star Nia gave me in my pocket. I take it out an look at it. Decidin to go all the way, I sneak into the back-stage door. I'm the one they use to handle the curtains at assemblies — why should this time be any diffrent? Luckily, Mr. Thayer was busy at the front doors. I almost trip over a dust mop an bump into Mr. Skye who chuckles an asks me where I'm goin.

"To man the curtains, sir!" I salute. I know he ain gonna stop me or bust on me. Me an him cool like that. Mr. George Skye knows I'm not gonna do nothin wrong. He continues on his way even though he'd already pulled the curtains back. I hide behind them at the spot where I can see the stage an peek at the audience. The auditorium gets quiet as the crowd watches Ms. Drench march down the center aisle and up to a microphone on-stage.

"Good morning parents and guardians! Welcome to

Gillespie School! I have spoken with some of you regarding your questions about a *gifted child* in Ms. Winston's sixth grade homeroom. It is *indeed* true. This child has the ability to make our students do better work *just by touching pencils.*"

Some people laugh nervously. Ms. Drench continues:

"I like to think of it as a *blessing* for our school." She lets that settle in for a moment. "No harm has been done, no laws have been broken. I realize that it must be a *little frightening* to know of a child with such power. However, she is an excellent student and very intelligent. She gets along well with everyone and we get a lot of services from her: Future Teacher, Class Messenger, artist, writer, Science Club member and — most importantly — *magic pencils*! Her class is nearby and I am asking that she be brought in so you may meet her."

She nods to Ms. Jett — the security guard, to get Nia. *Might as well be on TV*, I think. I'm a lil scared for Nia. I finger the star in my pocket. I look for Nia's mother an don't see her. Maybe her father came? My mother tol me she most likely wouldn't be able to make it. I don't see her or my dad.

The guard walks Nia in the back way, right by me. We touch hands an that seems to make us both feel better.

Then Ms. Drench says:

"Please bring the child onto the stage, Ms. Jett."

As Nia is brought out the audience responds wit:

"She's really small!"

"Awww, she's cute."

"Makin mah child look bad!"

"What gives her the power?"

"She ought a be shamed a herself, causin us to worry."

"Lessee what she got to say."

"Some kids have been calling her a witch!"

"I hear she moves things wit her eyes."

"They say she got boys under her control!"

"What kinda hair is that on her head?"

"How can we protect our children?"

"I don't believe any of this."

"This ain no school for hocus-pocus!"

On an on they mutter until Ms. Drench orders Nia to introduce herself an to say a few words. Nia hesitates then takes the mike:

"Hello everyone. My name is Nia Stellar." The crowd is quiet. Nia bravely goes on:

"I am ten years old and in the sixth grade. I like to help in the ways I can and I never meant to upset anyone. Unfortunately, most people become uncomfortable with my influence, so I move around a lot attending different schools. I will be leaving Gil—."

The principal leans toward Nia an snatches the mike from her.

"I ask you — parents and guardians — is this sweet child someone to fear?" She purrs. "All she has done is share her gifts with us. Our school will be among the best of the district *because of her!* Now I hope that any misinformation and worry has been laid to rest. Think of today as any other day at *Gillespie School!*

As *always*, we are looking for volunteers. Mr. Thayer — the Assistant Principal — will be taking names and phone numbers of those who would like to help. Mr. Thayer, please raise your hand. We *welcome* your participation. Thank you *so much* for coming!"

For some reason, the crowd don't take the hint to leave. It kinda looks like a circus freak show the way some folks are starin at Nia.

One man hollers:

"I'm takin my children out a here *today*! We don't know what else this girl can do!"

He pushes through the doors an a lotta other people follow behind him.

Meanwhile, Ms. Drench is askin everybody to remain calm an not to disrup the classes. Nia — still standin between the principal an Ms. Jett — is lookin calm. A woman comes to the stage an screams out that Nia is the *Antichrist!* This stops some a the flow from the auditorium. Other people begin to yell threats while some work theyselves into such a state that they kneel down an pray. Some begin to cuss or cry. A baby wails. Some a those who had left return wit they kids. The auditorium is packed now. Nia looks back at me. I make a weak smile an hold up my fist an say, "Stay strong!"

Lil did I know, Nia ain scared an she ain bowed. She stretches out her arms *an begins to glow!* I blink my eyes an look again. Yep, gleamin just like the pencil she gave me did! I realize then I had never heard nobody else say they pencil glowed. Maybe I *didn't* imagine that! But I couldn't think bout it now. The crowd notices Nia's glow an gets mystified an silent.

All eyes on Nia.

Now, I ain never messed wit no drugs but I sho feel like I've had somethin! I can't believe what I see: Nia stretchin taller an taller until her body floats an she's glowin like a great star! I can barely make out her face. It's as if she has become pure light! I feel somebody breathin on my neck an I turn around an face Martin! Guess he heard bout this in the neighborhood. We continue to witness the event together.

Nia speaks in a serious an deeper voice than ever before:

"I came to your school as I do to all schools. I inspired your children to do their best and — no one — not one among you fully believes your child is the one who improved her or his grades. Instead, you assume it was because I touched pencils. It was not I. It was *your child* feeling that he or she had some special power — and believing in that — behaving in the manner of all who wish to contribute their best.

But how can you keep expecting children to believe in themselves when their closest role models have no belief for them?

Ev-e-ry-child can learn.

Learning and abilities come in many forms. Not everyone can be the best in math, English and science. Some are geniuses with a football, verbal communication, entertainment, or a paintbrush. Some learn best through seeing, hearing, touching or doing. This is *basic*, something we all should know by now! It is not just about the pencil and the paper, nor just about the writing and the reading. It is about believing you are able to do what you can, then doing it, and using it to your advantage. Your strengths will overcome your weaknesses and you will begin reaching your *personal best.*"

By now, everybody is standin like statues as Nia's form continues to gleam over them. She speaks again:

"I am a *Seeker.* I search for places where the inhabitants need uplifting and empowerment. There are so many places on this planet that do, it will not be hard for me to offer my services again. I have made my mark at this place. It is time for me to move on and for all of you to return to your lives as if you never knew of me. But *I* will remember and so will a *Special One* here today."

Nia's gettin smaller now but still floatin overhead. She points to me an commands:

"Malcolm Bakersfield — you who are named after Malcolm X! What were his other three names during his lifetime of change?"

I thought she'd forgotten bout that. I step onto the stage an say: "Malcolm Little, Detroit Red, and El Hajj Malik El Shabazz!" Nia dips toward me.

"I name you *Hodari*, which in Kiswahili means *powerful.*

With you, I entrust my memory as you too will become a Seeker one day. Even now you are growing too powerful for this world." She waves her body back toward the crowd.

"As for the rest of you — and anyone else who knows of me — you will forget all but your children shall keep the skills they have developed. My *purpose* is to leave places I visit for the better. I give to *all* of you *diamonds in the rough* to nurture and refine as you come to understand that knowledge is nothing to be afraid of or ashamed of pursuing. But it requires belief, effort, and persistence in order to be constantly acquired. *The brilliance is in all of you!* But *you* must allow it to come through! Learn *five* new things everyday! Put aside any negative experiences and attitudes involving education — for the children's sakes. Help them to conquer where you may have failed. Work *with* the educators and administrators and *insist* they work with you. Do all you can to aid the children in their quest for knowledge.

Be a mentor to another's child because sometimes a non-relative can help where family cannot. Focus on the purpose; be positive. Learn to be a community again! Together you will be building young minds to be strong and to perform at their finest!"

Nia pauses, again wavin my way an says:

"And you — Hodari — for you I will be a favorite dream that you will learn to tell in your own time. You have shown me love and understanding. As always, I challenge you to become your best self and to follow your dreams. *Remember me as a dream, my brother.*"

"*I will, my sister!*" I whisper.

Nia becomes even smaller an less bright. The crowd gasps in awe as she becomes a sliver a light. *She flies right through me — an is gone!*

I touch my star.

It touches me.

Epilogue

Aw, man, Malc! Martin, what we gon do wit lil ole Malcolm, man? He the tallest taleteller I ever met!" Ole Jess exclaims; his friendly face framed by the sun.

"Naw, man, it's what Malc gon do wit us! Ain nothin wrong wit him. He know where he goin. So, do we gotstuh call you *Hodari* now?"

"Sho, if you wanna. *Happy birthday* brotha man!" I grin an touch Martin on the arm. "See you at six?"

"Ah'ight, *Hodari!*" Martin answers half-seriously. I like the sound of the name.

I turn round an start to take off on my bike when I hear Ole Jess say:

"Your brotha's a *powerful somethin* to be so young."

"I *heard* that, Jesse! Runs in the famly, you know." Martin drawls like he's 49 instead a nineteen.

I start pedalin an feel warm inside cuz *I believe they right.*

Author's Note

The characters of "The Magic Pencil" communicate effectively with one another in English but also by using varying colloquialisms. Most are following what some would call 'code switching.' I believe this behavior occurs in all people and cultures and that many do so with little or no effort as the situation necessitates. Of course, this is also true for black/African Americans. As the story's main characters are members of that group, the focus is on some of the group's colloquialisms.

For some it may seem impossible to switch back and forth due to how the language was spoken in their homes or how well the speakers fared, verbally, in standard English studies. Other variables would be socialization, wealth, influence from regions of the country, and the world. However, difficulty in switching can have nothing to do with intelligence or ability.

The characters' language styles are based on what I have experienced during my lifetime. Therefore, I am providing some examples and explanations: The reader will find more than one way to speak or use a word depending on which character is speaking. The reader will notice that the use of the suffix '-ing' (i.e., 'everything') is at the end of some words but ending with '-in' (i.e., 'cookin') on others. I chose to use the '-ing' pronunciation as opposed to the pronunciation of '-ang' (i.e., 'thing/thang') that some of the characters may have used in real life. I also chose to use apostrophes sparingly.

I grew up in a family where my sister, brothers and I all attended parochial schools, at least through the eighth grade. In them, we continued to learn to speak *"proper"* English and it was enforced and exhibited at home. However, our way of speaking with friends and neighbors was heavily influenced by the casual nature of our surroundings. While in school, we very same students, who excelled in standard English, both spoken and written, changed our inflections and mannerisms once away from the teachers' disapproving eyes and ears. Even then, before knowing of the term, we knew we were bilingual. Despite the attempts of others to cause such, we felt no stigma in speaking either way. Our world was widened by our ability to do so.

The method of communication is not a static thing. From cave paintings to hieroglyphics, Morse code to rap lyrics, all are legitimate in their own ways and times. The language of the people, not the editors, changes the entries in dictionaries.

Therefore, I thank a few of our literary warriors: James Baldwin, Amiri Baraka, Claude Brown, Paul Laurence Dunbar, Nikki Giovanni, Gloria Aneb House, Langston Hughes, Zora Neale Hurston, Toni Morrison, Walter Mosley, Ntozake Shange, Geneva Smitherman, Alice Walker, and Richard Wright for portraying the many shades of speech black people use, and have used, which spice up our American melting pot.

"Nothing in life is to be feared. It is only to be understood."
~ *Madame Marie Curie*

CREDITS

Akeelah and the Bee. . . motion picture, 2006, director Doug Atchison

"Black Family Pledge" . . . . Dr. Maya Angelou

The Brother from Another Planet. . . . . . .motion picture, 1984, director John Sayles

Finding Forrester . . . . . . motion picture, 2000, director Gus VanSant

"This Gift" . . . . Hayes G. Dabney, Sr., Esq., 1964

"Grazing in the Grass". . . .audio recording, 1968, performed by Hugh Masekela

Kung Fu Hustle . . . . motion picture, 2005, director Stephen Chow

Malcolm X . . . . . . .motion picture, 1992, director Spike Lee

"Nguzo Saba: The Seven Principles" . . Dr. Maulana Karenga

Quote after Author's Note . . . . .Madame Marie Curie

Sarafina. . . . motion picture, 1992, director Darrell J. Roodt

Scrabble . . . . Selchow and Righter

"Skeleton Parade". . . . . poem by Jack Prelutsky

Spiderman, The Silver Surfer, The Black Panther . . . .Marvel Comics

The Three Stooges . . . . C3 Entertainment, Inc.

X-Box. . . . . MSN Tech Games

Ordering Information

Mail Orders: Dabs & Company, PO Box 47327, Oak Park, MI 48237-5027, USA

Checks or money orders made payable to Karen E. Dabney

U.S.: $14.95 per book. $4.00 for shipping, add $2.00 for each additional book.

International: $14.95 per book. $9.00 for shipping, add $5.00 for each additional book.

Telephone: 313-632-3384 Facsimile: 313-341-7571

dabsandco@att.net

www.dabsandcompany.com

Name: _____

Address: _____

City: _____ State: _____ Zip: _____

Country: _____

Telephone(s): _____

e-mail address: _____

Method of payment:

☐ money order

☐ check

☐ I am interested in educational aids for *The Magic Pencil.*